Done In at the Dog Spa

Saltcliff Mysteries

Book 4

Nancy Stewart

Chapter One

Saltcliff on the Sea in the springtime was something I hadn't quite been prepared for. I'd enjoyed Saltcliff in the summer when I first arrived to take over the bed-and-breakfast—and guardianship of my niece—for my late sister, and I had enjoyed Saltcliff in the wintertime, despite the massive and unexpected ice storm that had kept us prisoner in the inn over the Christmas holiday.

My dog, Taco, had enjoyed every season in Saltcliff. But I think more than that, Taco Dog enjoyed our change in lifestyle and circumstances since moving to the small seaside town. He enjoyed the shift from our lives as defense contractors to the quieter, more leisurely life that came with running an inn in a small coastal California village and raising a twelve-year-old girl.

"The garden is coming along, Dahlia," announced

Marcus, stepping into the lobby as the bright March morning sunlight flooded in behind him.

"Well, I don't suppose it could get worse than it was." I shook my head sadly, thinking of the destruction that had befallen my sister's beautiful garden out front after an incident last fall. Luckily, Marcus was more than equipped to restore Daisy's beloved garden to its original beauty.

I was just gathering my things to take Taco Dog for his morning walk around the village when Diantha popped through the door that separated our apartment from the inn's lobby. She had an odd look on her face that I couldn't decipher. Her dark hair was pulled back into a ponytail, putting the heart shape of her beautiful face on display. Her eyes danced with something like mischief as she looked between me and Taco.

"Taking Taco for a walk?" She bounced on her toes.

Ripped jeans and a sweatshirt were a stark change from the wardrobe my niece had favored when I arrived. Gone were the ripped tights, all-black attire, and chunky eyeliner. She was a fresh-faced version of my twin sister— younger, full of optimism, and, strangely, suddenly interested in my morning routine with Taco Dog.

"Yep, just like every other morning." I said this with a bit of a question in my voice. She was not often out of bed before eleven if she didn't need to be, and it was spring break. Something was up.

"Do you think you'll be long?"

Again, odd interest. "Forgive me for saying so, but you don't normally seem to care about my walks with Taco in the mornings. You're not usually even out of bed at this hour unless you have school," I commented. "What's going on?"

"Well," my niece hedged, her fingers twisting together as if there was something she didn't want to tell me. "You see, there's a thing happening soon. And I thought... Taco would probably like to be a part of it."

"That's cryptic. And Taco's desires are pretty limited. He hasn't mentioned anything other than breakfast and a walk today."

I glanced at Marcus, who was still standing near the front door, chuckling as he watched this interaction.

"You're good at puzzles, Dahlia," he said to me. "You don't know what she's talking about?"

"Afraid not. I'm going to need a little more, Danny."

I snapped Taco's leash onto his collar. Regardless of whatever it was she was trying to say, Taco still needed to go outside.

"Since you're up, and you clearly have something you're having trouble saying, why don't you come for a walk with us and see if you can ask me on the way?"

Diantha nodded eagerly and stepped toward the front door as if about to head out.

I waited, hoping she might notice on her own that she

was not wearing shoes, but it seemed that twelve-year-olds had more important things on their minds.

"I think shoes might be in order," I told her.

My niece slapped her head dramatically and then skipped back through the door between the apartment and the lobby. A few minutes later, she returned, now properly shod.

"Let's go," I said, sending Taco into a spiral of excitement, bouncing at my feet as we moved toward the front door of the inn at last.

We headed out toward Ginger Street, the dappled sunshine of the morning filtering through the towering pine and eucalyptus trees, making the streets of Saltcliff gleam in the morning dew. The scent of brine was heavy in the air, blown up by the sea breeze from the beach just a few blocks away. I also caught hints of wild mustard, California lilac, and the lupine that were all in early bloom here on the Central Coast.

"So what is this thing that you don't want to tell me about? That involves my dog?"

"Well, you're making it sound so nefarious," Diantha said, impressing me with a word I didn't know she had in her vocabulary.

"Not nefarious, just mysterious."

"Well," she said, finally ready to tell me whatever this thing was, "you know the annual Saltcliff Dog Show will be in town next weekend."

I did not know that, but I wasn't at all surprised to hear that a town like Saltcliff on the Sea—which was extremely fond of its furry friends—would play host to a dog show every year.

"Anyway, I was hoping that you would let me enter Taco. And I thought I might teach him a trick or two to show off at the event. You know, to up his chances of winning."

I glanced down at my chocolate English Lab. He was beautiful, at least in my eyes. More than that, he was my best friend. He also had the rather important job of saving my life now and then, since he was a trained allergen dog who kept me from eating anything that might kill me—something I appreciated very much.

I considered Taco, trying to keep the skepticism from my voice. "What kind of trick are we talking about?"

Taco was excellent at his job, and there were many who would say that the ability for a Labrador to sniff out legumes was indeed a trick—and an impressive one at that. However, I had tried in the past to teach Taco simple tricks, like shake or play dead, with very little success. Like me, my dog seemed to be exceptionally task oriented. He did not see the purpose, perhaps, of shaking or playing dead. Of course, for a treat, he was willing to try.

"Taco Dog is super smart." Diantha proclaimed this as if I might disagree. "And I know he can learn anything we want to teach him."

I did not want to deflate the exceptional optimism in my niece's voice.

"Of course," I said. "I'm just curious what this trick will be."

"Well, I have a couple of ideas. But I was hoping Taco would have some time today to work through them with me."

I looked between my dog and my niece as we strolled beneath the overhanging branches on the main street of Saltcliff. There was a feeling I couldn't quite describe rising inside me. It was a mix between happiness and something so far beyond happiness that I couldn't find a name for it. My life had become something I had never imagined it would be, and seeing my beloved dog and my equally beloved niece bonding in this way filled me with this odd emotion. It was so big, I worried I wouldn't be able to contain it.

I swallowed, trying to keep the feeling inside, and said, "Of course you can. I don't think Taco has a lot of pressing plans for the day."

Diantha's hands clasped together as she smiled broadly. We walked a moment more and I drew to a stop in front of a pastel pink storefront. "Oh," I said, remembering that Taco did, in fact, have plans today. "Actually, Taco has a grooming appointment today at the Paw Spa."

I pointed at the building we were standing next to. Diantha's eyes grew large as she looked between me and the very fancy pink Paw Spa, where the pets of Saltcliff were bathed, primped, and pampered in ways that Taco had certainly never been.

"You made Taco an appointment at the Paw Spa?" Diantha's voice held all the skepticism mine would have had if I had told myself that even a month ago.

"Yes. Amal and Nina Reyes are old friends, and when she introduced me a couple of weeks ago, Nina suggested that Taco could benefit from a shedding treatment and an exfoliation, along with a quick nail grind. And I couldn't really disagree."

As I spoke, tufts of fur seemed to be ejecting themselves spontaneously from Taco's newly erupting spring coat.

Diantha peered through the plate-glass window of the Paw Spa. "It sure looks fancy."

"It is," I assured her, casting a dubious glance at my decidedly un-fancy dog.

Taco had certainly never been pampered in the way he was about to be pampered, and I only hoped he didn't cause a commotion and embarrass us all. The price alone told me this was probably the one and only time Taco would get such a treatment. I certainly hoped he would enjoy it.

Just as Diantha and I turned to proceed on our walk, the Paw Spa door burst open, and we were nearly run over by two people embroiled in loud conversation and a large white dog on a diamond-studded leash.

The man and woman stopped practically on top of us on the sidewalk, while the dog paused to give Taco a hello sniff.

"Camille, please," the man said in a beseeching tone, his hands pressed together against his chest in a prayer. "The show is just around the corner. This is no time to make rash decisions."

I tugged Diantha to one side of the sidewalk, just slightly out of the way, but the arguing couple seemed in no hurry to move along, and the dogs seemed to have fallen deep into dog conversation, taking turns sniffing various parts of one another and jigging playfully from side to side.

"That's enough, Lou. I've made my decision," the woman shrilled. She wore a pink skirt suit that even I could recognize as Chanel, carried a huge purse that might have been a Birkin bag, and wore heels I was fairly certain would be a safety hazard on the uneven sidewalks of Salt-cliff. "I cannot take another moment of the casual lack of professionalism you've displayed one too many times when working with Beaumont." The woman glanced at her dog as she said this, seeming to notice only then that the dog was having his own social interaction.

"Beaumont, come away at once!" The woman lifted her head and glared at me. "Can't you control your flea-ridden mutt?"

"Um." Words failed me. For one thing, I had not expected to be shouted at first thing in the morning by an overdressed stranger, and for another, I was exceptionally offended on Taco's behalf. I was about to respond, but Diantha had already stepped between the woman and me.

"Taco is a purebred English Labrador Retriever," she said haughtily. "And he does not have fleas!"

"Danny," I whispered, secretly glad she'd jumped to Taco's defense but feeling certain I was supposed to be teaching her not to shout at strangers, even if they were rude.

"That makes him no less common, young lady. And now Beau will need to be groomed all over again, since your... dog... seems to have salivated all over him." The woman sniffed and gave Beau's leash a mighty tug, and then the two of them were off and down the sidewalk.

Taco gave me a searching look with dolefully sad eyes, the excited saliva still dripping from his jowls.

"It's okay, buddy," I assured him, giving him a quick pat.

The man with whom the woman had been arguing stood still, rubbing his jaw with one hand as if he hadn't quite recovered from being yelled at himself. He seemed to start as he caught my eye, like he'd only just realized we were still there, and then his eyes landed on Taco.

"Well, that's a handsome dog you've got there," he said,

extended his knuckles toward Taco to sniff. "Mind if I pet him?" he asked me.

"Sure," I said, glad someone seemed to admire my dog. Taco sat happily and let the man lavish his ears and head with pats and expressions of admiration.

"Great example of his breed," the man said. "English?"

"Yes," I agreed. Diantha stepped closer to Taco.

"Don't listen to Camille," he said, motioning behind him to the fancy woman who'd stormed away. "She thinks her Borzoi Beau is the only dog worth talking about."

Aha, a Borzoi. I hadn't recognized the breed right away, but he was certainly unique.

"Is she in town for the dog show?" Diantha asked him.

The man grimaced as if talk of the dog show was painful for him. "Unfortunately, yes. She lives here part time, spring and summer. I used to work for her—I was Beau's handler when he showed. Until today."

"Oh, I'm sorry," I said. Then, feeling slightly rude, I extended a hand. "I'm Dahlia Vale, and this is my niece, Diantha. And Taco Dog. We run the Saltcliff Bed and Breakfast."

"Ah, yeah, I've walked by there. It's a nice place," the man said. He shook my hand. "Lou Grant. Don't suppose you're in the market for a handler for the show, are you?"

Diantha looked at me with a worried expression.

"No thanks, Lou," I told him. "Danny here will be Taco's handler for the show this year."

He nodded, a rueful smile on his face. "Well, I wish you the best of luck. You probably already know this, but Beau wins every year."

Diantha's face fell. "You mean it's fixed?"

He shook his head. "I wouldn't say that, kid. But Beau was bred to win shows. His full name is Beaumont Royale, if you can swallow that. He's from a champion line, and Camille Hawthorne rubs shoulders with all the right people, if you get my drift."

I did not really "get his drift," but I understood that Beau the Borzoi was favored to win.

"Taco here has a good shot at Best in Breed, I'd say," he told us, reaching down to give Taco's ruff another good rub. Taco seemed very pleased at either the news or the attention. Maybe both.

"Hear that?" Diantha asked me.

"I did," I assured her. "Well, thanks for the information, Mr. Grant. We wish you luck finding another engagement soon."

"Nice meeting you," he said, wandering somewhat forlornly down the sidewalk.

Chapter Two

That afternoon, Taco Dog and I returned to the Paw Spa. While there were no arguing couples outside, the spa was a hive of dog-pampering activity. Taco and I entered, both of us fascinated by the movement and excitement inside the small salon.

Against one wall were several shower-tub fixtures, where employees—or possibly owners—were using hand-held nozzle showerheads to wash dogs of various sizes. Tucked into a side room, just visible from the door, was a huge tub where an enormous dog was being lathered up by a woman with dark hair pulled into a high ponytail. Behind a glass window, several dogs stood on high tables as groomers brushed them, blow-dried them, or applied any number of lotions and oils to their fur. There were more dogs in one place than I had ever seen before. And more owners chattering to one another than I had ever hoped to see. It was all a bit overwhelming.

Taco shivered with delight and excitement as he valiantly practiced his self-restraint. I knew he would've loved to gallop from table to table, greeting all the other dogs, but he did not. Maybe Diantha had a chance of teaching him a trick after all, I thought.

A few moments after we entered, the woman at the big tub in the back stood from her seat atop a metal stool, dried her hands, and approached us with a friendly smile. I recognized her as Nina, the spa owner, whom Amal had briefly introduced me to previously.

"Dahlia, Taco! You're here. We are so happy to have you at the Paw Spa." Nina greeted Taco as if he deserved an equal amount of attention as any human in the room. Personally, I appreciated this very much.

"I hadn't realized you would be so busy today. I wasn't aware of the dog show until just this morning," I told her, looking around and feeling slightly nervous amid all the activity.

"No problem," she assured me. "The busier, the better. Yes, we have lots of champion dogs coming through these days, but we always make time for local dogs—they're my bread and butter." Nina seemed excited about this, so I didn't bother suggesting that we might come back another day when they were less busy.

I was about to hand over Taco's leash, once I had established that she was ready for him, when a loud voice came from one of the washing areas to our left.

"You know that none of that is true!" a woman cried loudly.

Nina glanced at me, worried, and gave me a half smile.

The woman continued. "It's all been disproven. I can't believe this is still a problem, when BoBo Jingles was 100 percent cleared at the Babbington Dog Show last May."

The woman at whom this defense was directed was also washing a dog at the far side of the room. She had curly dark hair and very bright lipstick.

"I didn't mean anything by it, Victoria," she replied. "Only that Camille mentioned it again yesterday."

Victoria, whom I gathered was the woman with long red hair washing BoBo Jingles—a very small white dog—in the tub before her, rolled her eyes.

"I have had just about enough of Camille Hawthorne," she said. "That woman is the scourge of the circuit, and she needs to mind her own business. Plus, Beaumont Royale is not that special."

"I wouldn't blame this on Beau," said the other woman. "After all, he is a confirmed champion."

"I see how you slipped the word *confirmed* in there so slyly." Victoria did not sound particularly pleased, and I wondered what the word *confirmed* meant in this situation. The discussion—or argument—continued, but Nina had taken my elbow and was drawing me back toward the large tub.

"Don't pay any attention," she said.

The head of the enormous dog waiting patiently beneath a coat of lather in the back tub turned toward us. He was a tricolor dog—a Greater Swiss Mountain Dog, I guessed—and he was beautiful. "Is this dog going to be in the show?" I asked Nina.

She grinned at the Greater Swiss Mountain dog. "She sure is. Her name is Moxie."

Moxie nodded at me, as if acknowledging these facts.

"Hello Moxie," I said.

"Moxie is another champion in town for the show. As for the thing Victoria was going on about over there..." she shook her head. "Dog show people are very petty about things like bloodlines and studs. And there was a bit of a question a while back about BoBo Jingles's bloodline."

"A question?" I asked, interested in this new world I had never been exposed to. Taco Dog was purebred, but I had never concerned myself with his bloodline. I only needed his nose to work properly.

"Well, Victoria is a breeder of Bichon Frisés. A couple of years ago, she had a litter that she was selling, and there was some question about the authenticity of her documentation."

"What do you mean?" I asked.

"Well, in order for dogs to compete in shows at a

certain level, they must come from a certified stud. And there were some whispers that Victoria's stud was not properly documented—which meant her litter was also potentially not documented. But when questioned, she came up with some papers, so I guess it all worked out in the end."

Victoria was still railing at the woman next to her about how petty discrepancies were better left in the past. "She still seems very upset," I commented.

"Well, Camille Hawthorne was here earlier, and she likes to stir the pot. So I think Victoria is feeling a bit sensitive right now. Dog show people have long memories, and Victoria will probably always battle the questions about her reputation."

I thought about that—about the way what other people thought of you could affect the way you were treated, even the way you thought about yourself.

"Poor Victoria," I said aloud, wondering if she deserved any of the suspicion that was clearly aimed her way.

"Poor Victoria, indeed," Nina agreed, rinsing the lather from the Swiss Mountain Dog in the tub as Taco and I watched. "She needs a win this year, or she may be done."

I stared at her, not quite sure what she meant. Nina read the confusion on my face.

"I hate to gossip, but it's pretty widely known that If Victoria doesn't win the Saltcliff Dog Show, she will likely have to find another career. I've heard rumors that she's out of money, and there's very little demand for her dogs at this point, with all the controversy and everything."

"Who knew the world of dogs was this complicated?" I thought aloud.

"You don't know the half of it," Nina commented, rolling her eyes. "The world of dogs is cutthroat and competitive. Everyone is constantly trying to get dirt on everyone else, and I've even heard rumors of sabotage and bribery." She shook her head as if this was too much to even speak about.

"Earlier, someone told us that Camille and her dog, Beau, always wins," I said. "You don't think she's bribing anyone, do you?"

Nina paused in her work, rinsing off the big dog in the tub. She busied herself for a moment, not answering the question. But then she cleared her throat and said, "Between you, me, and the doorpost? I certainly wouldn't put it past her. Camille knows how to play the game like nobody else. Add to that the fact that she's completely paranoid and, frankly, evil, and I'd say it's likely."

Well, that didn't sound good. I'd need to let Diantha know exactly what she was getting into. Of course, Taco wasn't going to be competing against the pedigreed dogs. For Diantha and Taco, it would just be for fun.

For Victoria, Camille, and Beau, though, it sounded like life and death.

"Is Taco ready for his treatment?" Nina asked me, reaching for Taco's leash.

I suddenly felt nervous about leaving my best friend in a place that now reminded me an awful lot of the lunchroom back in middle school—people whispering behind your back and spreading rumors. Would Taco be okay here?

Nina must've read my reluctance, because she said, "He'll have the time of his life, Dahlia. And you're welcome to stay, if you like."

I glanced down at Taco, who was gazing around excitedly, his tongue lolling out one side of his open mouth. He would be fine, I decided. He was a beautiful, confident dog—nothing like the kid I was thinking of back in that school lunchroom. People had been cruel to that kid, but people only said nice things to Taco Dog.

I handed Nina his leash and squatted down to give my friend a good rub and a quick kiss on the nose. "I'll be back soon," I promised him. "How long do you think it will be?" I asked.

Nina checked her watch. "He should be finished this afternoon around four," she said. "But if you'd like to leave him overnight, I have some boarding spots in the back and I can check if I have an opening. I'll give him dinner and he'll get a walk too."

"Oh no, that's okay," I said, hating the idea of Taco staying overnight here and having to wonder why I hadn't come back for him. "I'll be back for him, or I'll send my niece Danny."

"Sounds good!" Nina returned her attention to Taco, who she walked through a door into the back, and I made my way back out to the street.

On my way back to the inn, I felt oddly lonely without Taco at my side, but I was greeted by Amal's wide smile when I stepped through the front door into the lobby.

Over the months since I had taken on guardianship of both my niece and my sister's inn, Amal and I had become quite close. This was novel, since I had never really had close friends before. I had had colleagues, and I had had my sister. But since my sister Daisy and I had not spoken in about ten years, I didn't think I could count her among my friends. Amal's bright smile and graceful acceptance of my less attractive qualities sent a warm rush through me as I pulled the door shut behind me.

"Taco off being pampered?" Amal asked.

"He is," I told her. "I just hope he enjoys himself. There was so much activity at the Paw Spa."

"Yes, the annual Saltcliff Dog Show. Danny tells me she has big plans for Taco."

"She does. I just hope he won't disappoint her in his ability to learn new tricks." I hated seeing my niece upset. I couldn't imagine being an actual parent, especially to the youngest of children. Toddlers were so often thwarted by the oversized world of adults. It would be terrible watching them constantly upset. Not to mention all the noise they made.

"Taco's not that old of a dog," Amal commented. "And he's pretty smart. I think they'll do fine."

I had just joined her behind the reception desk and was beginning to review a stack of mail set to one side when the lobby door opened again. We were checking in two guests today, and since only one of them was a man— and a man had just stepped in—I assumed it must be Mr. Elliott Nazar.

The man who had just come inside looked around himself with appraising eyes. He had a scruff of gray hair covering his jaw and another at the top of his head, and wore a royal blue scarf wound multiple times around his rather long neck. He shuffled forward, turning his appraisal on Amal and me, and then said in a rather too loud voice, "Checking in."

I tended to be taken aback by anything that didn't fit my expectations for how people might behave, and thus, I stared at him for what was probably too long. Amal, as she often did, stepped in. "Mr. Nazar?" she asked.

"That's me," he said, offering his ID and credit card.

"We have you set up in the Gatsby Suite," Amal said. "I think you'll find it wonderful, but if you have any issues, please do let us know. I'm Amal, the manager, and this is Dahlia, the inn's proprietor."

Proprietor was not the word I would have chosen for myself, especially because technically, the inn belonged to my niece. However, it worked for now—introducing a twelve-year-old as the owner would probably only raise additional questions from Mr. Nazar.

"I'm sure it will be fine," he said gruffly, accepting the key. As he did so, a gold-linked chain bracelet slipped from the sleeve of his shirt and rested against his outstretched hand. It was at odds with the rest of his old money look in its gleaming, over-the-top style. He shoved it back into his sleeve as he dropped his arm.

"You'll be staying with us just over a week?" Amal looked up at him to confirm.

"Yes. Here for the show next weekend. I'll be headed out straightaway after it's over."

That piqued my interest. "But you don't have a dog with you," I pointed out.

Mr. Nazar squinted at me in a less-than-friendly fashion before saying, "I do not own dogs. I critique them."

"I didn't know that *dog critic* was a job," I said, wishing I could retract the words the second they were out of my mouth.

He continued to sneer at me, and I realized that he was

yet another of the many personalities who populated the world of professional dog showing—or at least the world of the Saltcliff Annual Dog Show.

"I am one of the judges," Mr. Nazar explained in a flat tone.

I had very little to add and was somewhat relieved when he took his suitcase to the stairs as Amal directed him to his room.

The other guest, who I assumed was probably also involved with the dog show, would not be joining us until later that afternoon.

When Amal returned from showing Mr. Nazar to his room, I told her that I was going to get a start on the baking for tomorrow morning, then headed through the door to the apartment that adjoined the hotel lobby.

"Sounds good," she called.

Chapter Three

Inside the apartment, I found Diantha lying on her stomach in the center of the living room with a laptop in front of her.

"What are you doing?" I asked her. School was out for a week, I hadn't expected to find her working on anything.

"Research. I need to learn everything there is to know about dog shows," she said. "I wanna make sure Taco Dog has the best possible chance of winning."

I didn't want to let my niece down, but I also didn't want her to believe that Taco Dog would be competing against the likes of Beaumont Royale. "Danny, you do realize that Taco will be competing in a different category than the champion dogs, don't you?"

"Of course, Aunt Dolly," she laughed. "But that doesn't mean I don't want him to have the very best chance of winning."

I shrugged, happy if she was happy, and headed for the kitchen.

As soon as I was elbow-deep in my first batch of scones, my phone dinged on the counter where I had left it. I glanced at it, not wanting to get flour all over the screen, and saw that it was a text from Owen Sanderson.

I tried to repress the giddy excitement that flooded me every time I saw his name appear on my phone. I was a grown-up, after all, and whatever lay between me and Detective Sanderson was also grown-up and mature. Giddiness and childish excitement had no place. Did they?

Of course, I had absolutely no experience in the world of adult relationships, and every time Owen smiled at me, I felt like a ten-year-old, unsure what to do with my appendages or my face. Still, none of that seemed to bother him, and he kept calling, texting, and even asking me on dates.

Owen: *Dahlia, wondering if you are busy the weekend after next? I would like to invite you to attend the Policeman's Ball in San Francisco with me.*

The nerves flared once again, and I pressed a hand hard against my ribs, as if I could contain the butterflies jumping to life inside me.

A ball. In San Francisco. As far as I knew only fairytale princesses went to balls. I had certainly never been to a ball. I *had* been to San Francisco before. But an evening event in San Francisco... would that require an overnight stay? My mind raced in circles with questions.

Dahlia: *That sounds exciting. Will you share details, please?*

Owen: *It's a formal event that includes dinner and dancing, and I expect that we would need to head up Friday afternoon and return home by noon on Saturday.*

A formal event would require formal attire. And while I had nothing that I thought would be appropriate, I was more worried about the overnight stay. I had kissed Owen before, but I knew that people spending the night together in hotel rooms had certain expectations, and I wasn't sure what Owen's expectations might be.

Still, I trusted him. And more than that, I knew that he understood better than most exactly who I was. He might have already guessed that my overnight experience with men was not extensive.

Dahlia: *I guess I should look for a dress.*

Owen: *So is that a yes?*

Dahlia: *It's a yes.*

I abandoned the scones and returned to the lobby, desperate to talk to Amal.

She was engaged, however, with our second guest for the evening—a woman with an extremely nervous French bulldog at her feet.

The bulldog was shivering with excitement, and when

it stood and moved to the other side of the woman's feet, I saw that it had left a small puddle on the floor.

"Oh my goodness, I'm so embarrassed." The woman's face turned from pale pink to a bright shade of red.

"It's not a problem," Amal assured her as I rushed to grab paper towels and the pet spray we kept below the sideboard at the side of the room. "We are a pet-friendly hotel, and when he is not busy getting groomed, we have a resident Labrador who usually welcomes all of our guests."

"Sir Edgar's just such a baby still," the woman said, waving a hand at the tiny French bulldog.

"Is Edgar competing next weekend?" I asked her.

"Oh no," she said. "He's too young yet. We're just here to get a sense of the competition. He'll be competing next spring... next fall, maybe."

"Dahlia, this is Emerson Sanford. She'll be staying with us through the week as well," Amal said.

"As well?" Emerson asked. "Is there someone else here for the dog show?"

"There is," Amal said. "One of the judges, I gather."

Emerson's mouth dropped open in a little O of surprise before she asked, "Is it Amelia Vanderbush? Or Selena Slate? Or is it Elliott Nazar?"

Amal and I exchanged a look. It was against our policy to share information about guests with anyone.

"I have no doubt you'll find out soon enough," Amal

said. "You'll both be down for breakfast in the morning, I'm sure."

With that, Amal helped Emerson and Sir Edgar to their quarters on the first floor. When she returned, I felt like I should make some sort of small talk or pleasant conversation before giving her my news, but I wasn't able to contain myself.

"Owen asked me out on a date. An overnight date to the Policeman's Ball in San Francisco. It's a formal event with dancing and dinner, and... probably a hotel." All of the words gushed out of my mouth in a torrent, and Amal's eyes grew wider and wider as I spoke.

"Dahlia, that sounds amazing," she said with a wide smile that steadied my nerves a bit.

"But, Amal... a hotel?"

"Don't get ahead of yourself, Dahlia," she said. She laid a reassuring hand on my shoulder. "I think Owen knows you need to come to things in your own time. I've no doubt there will be zero pressure from him."

I had told myself the same thing, but it was a relief to hear Amal say it too. Owen was a good man, and I believed he liked me for real reasons—though I often wasn't sure quite what they were. I knew only that I admired and respected him... and didn't mind the fact that he was extremely handsome, either.

I was about to dive into another round of what if questions with Amal when my cell phone pinged again. I pulled it from my pocket and glanced at the screen to see a text from Nina at the spa.

Paw Spa: *Taco is ready.*

Diantha and I went back to the Paw Spa to pick up Taco, eager to see him looking his very best after being pampered and primped.

"Oh, he looks so handsome," Diantha exclaimed when Taco was led out to greet us by Nina.

"He does," I agreed, impressed that Taco had allowed Nina to tie a jaunty neckerchief around his neck. It gave him an oddly Western look, like he might spend his days herding cows or something. But the shiny coat he sported did not look anything like that of a dog who spent long days on the range. I dropped down to pet Taco's head, murmuring softly in his ear.

"He did great," Nina was saying. "He did not particularly enjoy the blow dryer—"

"Oh no," Diantha said. "He hates the vacuum cleaner too. Loud noises, I guess."

"Well, we figured it out, we just—" Nina trailed off, her eyes on the front door.

Diantha and I turned to see what had caught her attention, only to find Camille Hawthorne and her prize Borzoi Beaumont Royale stepping in. What were the odds we'd have to bump into the woman twice in one day? I wanted to hide Taco so she couldn't say anything else disparaging about him, but she fixed her attention on Nina.

"You there. Anita," Camille barked.

"Camille. You know very well that my name is Nina," Nina said in an icy tone.

"There's been an unfortunate incident at my summer house, and it isn't safe for Beaumont to stay there this evening. I'll need him to board here with you." Camille held out Beau's leash as if this were a done deal.

"We are usually booked weeks in advance," Nina said, her tone only slightly warmer than before. I wondered at her statement, since she'd offered Taco an overnight stay just a few hours earlier.

"I'm sure you have room for him," Camille added in a haughty tone, thrusting the handle of the leash out once again. When Nina hesitated, Camille's eyes flitted to where I still knelt at Taco's side. I'd wrapped an arm around him, though I wasn't sure if I was seeking support or attempting to give it to him. "Oh. Hello again," Camille sniffed.

"I do have one large kennel available," Nina said, relenting. She took Beau's leash in hand, and the dog promptly moved to sit at her side, gazing up at her with affection.

"Excellent. He'll need a walk and he eats promptly at five-thirty. I've brought his food." She extracted a Ziplock baggie full of what looked like ground beef and carrots from her purse. "It must be refrigerated, of course. And then heated for him, but not too warm."

"Of course," Nina said in a dry tone.

"I'll be off, then," Camille said, turning on her heel to leave. She turned at the last moment. "Also, Nadine, could you see that Beau is kept as far from the common dogs as possible? The last thing we need is for him to pick up some nasty parasite just a week before the show." She cast a glance at Taco as she said this, and I hugged him tighter.

When Camille had left, Nina sighed deeply. "Sorry about that."

I stood, smoothing my pants and trying to regain my composure. Camille Hawthorne made me extremely uncomfortable.

Diantha leaned in. "You don't have parasites, do you, Taco Doggy?"

"Of course not. Ignore her," Nina said. "She's a piece of work, and if you want the truth, I've had just about enough of her."

She took Beaumont Royale to the back—for his part, Beau actually seemed like a very nice dog—and then she rang us up and we were on our way back to the inn.

"I bet Beau will have a nice night being away from awful Camille," Diantha said.

"Maybe so," I agreed.

Chapter Four

The following morning, Taco and I were out bright and early, enjoying the fresh air that seemed to be available in abundance along the winding side streets of the village. Normally, we would have let our usual route guide us, but my new fascination with all things related to dog shows must have influenced me subconsciously. Without meaning to, we found ourselves heading toward the Paw Spa.

We were just approaching the storefront when I heard a startling sound—something very unusual for early morning in our quiet village. Or really, probably, anywhere.

A bloodcurdling scream.

Taco and I exchanged a glance as if to ask each other, *Did you hear that?*

Then we were off, hurrying toward the front door of the spa.

Stepping inside, I found the place much quieter than it had been the previous afternoon. That said, chaos still reigned.

Nina Reyes stood at the door to the back room where the hydrotherapy tub was located. This time, the tub did not hold a Greater Swiss Mountain Dog. Taking a step closer, I moved past Nina's hyperventilating form to see that it held a woman's body instead. A woman in a pink Chanel suit.

"Oh my goodness. Oh my goodness. Oh my goodness." Nina chanted as I moved past her to see if I could save the woman whose body floated in the tub, pushed to and fro by the strong jets on either side. I put my fingers to Camille Hawthorne's throat, but I knew before I touched her clammy skin that she was gone.

Looking back at Nina, Taco still loyal at my side, I asked, "What happened?"

Nina's terrified eyes scanned the interior of her business as another employee stepped out from the grooming room. "Derek called me to tell me the front door was left unlocked."

The teenager who'd just stepped from the grooming room shrugged. "I didn't want her to blame me."

"And what were you doing here so early?" I asked, looking between them.

"I always come early to walk the boarding dogs," he said, his voice shaky.

"Derek, did you find Camille in the tub?" I asked.

He nodded his head. "Yes ma'am, I came in, and the second I found the door unlocked, I called Nina. Then I heard the hydrotherapy tub still running, and when I looked—" He swallowed hard.

I turned toward the tub again, my stomach lurching as I took in the scene—the jets still running, pushing Camille's body back and forth in the water.

"Can we turn that off?" I asked.

Nina shook her head, her eyes wide. "I can't... I can't go in there. I can't see her like that."

"I think we better call the police," I said, reaching for my phone.

Nina slumped to the ground, landing in a heap. She was sitting up, at least—I was grateful she hadn't passed out—but she did seem to be in shock. I crouched down and looked her in the eye. "Are you okay? I'm going to call the police, and they'll figure everything out."

"It's just... I haven't even told you everything yet."

I looked around and caught Derek's expression. He made a face halfway between a grimace and a wince, as if he already knew whatever it was Nina was about to say.

"What is it?" I pressed.

Nina swallowed hard. "Beaumont Royale," she said, her voice unsteady. "He's missing."

I blinked. "What?"

"When I went back to take care of the boarding dogs, I noticed his crate was open," Derek said. The boy walked to the front desk, retrieving something he held up for me to see. It was a diamond-studded collar—the exact match to the leash Camille had been holding the day before.

I stared at it, my mind racing. "Derek, did you touch anything?" I asked.

"No, ma'am," he said quickly. "Just this. I picked it up off the floor by his crate."

"Okay," I said, taking a breath. "Nobody touch anything that you haven't already touched. Actually, nobody touch anything at all. I'm calling the police, and they'll know what to do. We should all wait outside until they get here."

I stepped back out onto the sidewalk, helping Nina out, and then pulled out my phone to dial Owen's number. His voice was friendly and reassuring as he greeted me, but I could hear the shift in his tone when I said, "There's a body at the Paw Spa."

"I was hoping you were going to invite me for breakfast, but I guess we'll do this instead." A beat of silence, then, "You're there now?"

"Yes," I said. "There's a woman in the hydrotherapy tub. And I know a body does not equate to a murder, but there might be a few suspects, actually."

"I'll be there soon."

I stuffed my phone back into my pocket and turned toward Nina and Derek, who both looked like they were in a state of shock. I thought a warm cup of tea might help, but didn't want to leave them alone.

Glancing down the street to Tidal Beans Coffee, I was just considering whether it would be more helpful to stay with them or to go get some tea, when a familiar form appeared around the corner.

Sylvan, my friend and local gossip aficionado, approached with his Bassett Hound Luigi at his side. "Good morning, my friends!" Sylvan greeted us with wide arms and a big smile. "What are you doing out so early, handsome Taco?" he cooed, bending down to let Taco and Luigi sniff noses.

Though I usually appreciated Sylvan's dramatic flair, it seemed ill-fitting this morning. "The morning isn't so good actually," I told him.

"Everything is just a matter of perspective, you know that," he said with a wink.

"Except maybe murder," I muttered. Then, remembering that it wasn't officially a murder yet, I amended, "I mean, maybe it's not such a good day when someone is dead."

Sylvan's mouth dropped open dramatically, and he clutched his chest with a gasp. He looked from me to Derek and Nina, then whispered, "Who is it?"

"A dog breeder in town for the show, unfortunately," I

said. I gave him a moment to process this news before continuing. "I wondered if you might sit with Nina and Derek for just a minute while I get some tea for them?"

Sylvan sighed and placed a gentle hand on Nina's shoulder as he sank onto the bench at her side. "Poor thing," he murmured. "You found the body?" Nina let out a shaky breath and nodded. Sylvan patted her back comfortingly as I handed Taco's leash to him and jogged to the corner tea shop.

I returned a few moments later with two steaming cups of tea, hoping they would help calm Derek and Nina. Just as I handed them their cups, Owen pulled up in his car and stepped out, another officer at his side.

"Dahlia," Owen said, nodding at me and giving me a secret smile. Then he looked at Nina and Derek, sitting on the bench outside the spa.

"You two found the body?" he asked.

Nina nodded, letting out a shaky breath. "I did. This morning when I came in after Derek called me."

"And why did Derek call you?"

"Because the door was unlocked, sir." Derek sat up straighter, as if Owen might be grading him on his posture.

"And I'm just here for moral support," Sylvan said, standing and bowing dramatically to the police officers. "But I see you have it well in hand, and I will be on my way." He walked Luigi around the officers and down the sidewalk, waving above his head as he departed and calling loudly, "Ta-ta!"

Owen and the other officer disappeared inside the Paw Spa. I sat with Nina, who was getting a bit of color back in her cheeks. Derek, too, seemed to be recovering from the shock.

A few moments later, Owen came back outside and gestured for me to join him. I entered the shop, noticing that the hydrotherapy jets had finally been turned off. It was eerily silent inside without the chatter of customers and dogs filling the space. What a difference from the day before.

"So you were the first one here after they discovered the body?" Owen asked me.

I told him everything that had happened so far, beginning with the scream that Taco and I had heard on the sidewalk. "There is something else, though," I told him. "Camille's dog is missing."

"Camille is the woman in the tub," Owen confirmed, pointing toward the back room.

"Yes. And her dog, Beaumont Royale, was heavily favored to win the Saltcliff Dog Show next week."

"And you think someone stole him?" Owen asked, as I walked him to the open crate.

"I don't know what to think," I told him honestly. It did seem suspicious. "If he simply escaped, he took his collar off first and unlocked the door to get out."

"You did say he was a champion," Owen said, shooting me a half-smile.

"I don't think he is capable of unlocking a door," I said.

Owen chuckled. "Probably not. So maybe someone killed Camille to get to her dog?"

"I guess I'm just not sure what Camille would've been doing here in the first place," I told him. "Yesterday, she came in when I was getting Taco and said that Beau would need to spend the night here because of something going on at her house."

"We definitely have more questions than answers," Owen said, rubbing one hand across his square jaw.

We walked back toward the door, stopping for a moment to look into the room where the tub now stood silent, Camille's body floating peacefully in the water. I took one step closer, interested in something I'd just noticed.

"She has a mark on her face," I pointed out. There was a bruise and a bit of blood just above her right eye on her forehead and disappearing into her hairline.

"She does," Owen agreed, squinting as he leaned a bit closer. "I'll have the coroner check that out." Owen turned to exit, nearly tripping over the metal stool Nina had been sitting on when I'd been here the day before. It was on the floor now, on its side.

Soon, the Paw Spa was a hub of police activity. Investigators were processing the scene, and the coroner had arrived. There was no more reason for me to be there, so I said goodbye to Owen, wished Nina and Derek the best, and returned to the inn.

I was greeted just inside the door by a very enthusiastic Diantha. "There you are!" She was practically dancing a jig as I unlatched Taco's leash and hung it on his hook. "Amal said you took Taco for a walk, but you've been gone for *hours*."

"Yes, well, it was a very eventful walk."

I gave Diantha a hug and then relinquished Taco to her care so she could teach him whatever tricks she thought he could learn. Then I joined Amal in Elliott Nazar's room, where she was changing the sheets.

"You're not gonna believe this," Amal said, shaking her head as she stood up straight and stretched her back after leaning over the mattress to strip the bed.

"I think you just stole my line," I told her. "But tell me yours first."

"Mr. Nazar has already left us."

Surprise made me tilt my head at my friend. Mr. Nazar was supposed to be here through the dog show—that was his entire reason for visiting. "What? Why did he leave?"

Amal shrugged. "I have no idea. He was at the front desk almost as soon as you left to take Taco for a walk, telling me his plans had changed and he needed to check out immediately."

Well, that was very suspicious.

"That's interesting," I said, tucking the sheet on my side and giving it a good tug to get it flat. "There was a dog breeder found dead at the Paw Spa this morning."

Amal froze. She looked up at me with a question in her eyes, then straightened and tossed the final pillow onto the bed. "I think maybe you should've told me yours first."

I explained to her what had transpired that morning on my walk, then shared my suspicion. "I wonder if Mr. Nazar's sudden departure had anything to do with Camille's death."

Amal scratched her head and let out a sigh. "Dahlia, forgive me for saying this, but ever since you came to Salt-cliff, dead bodies seem to keep turning up everywhere."

"I assure you, I have very little to do with any of it."

As Amal gathered the dirty sheets and tidied up the rest of the room, she laughed. "Well, life here certainly has become a lot more interesting since you arrived."

I didn't know why bodies kept turning up, but I did know that this latest one might impact both the dog show and the Policeman's Ball.

Not to be selfish about it, of course.

Chapter Five

The evening was spent attending to our guest, sharing dinner with Diantha and Amal in the apartment, and reviewing the books for the week ahead. While I did each of these things, however, Camille's face kept coming back to me. I couldn't shake how she had looked floating in the tub at the Paw Spa.

She'd been pale, of course—most dead people were, I supposed—but it seemed like she had also looked *frightened.* I knew it was irrational for me to assign emotion to a dead woman, but I couldn't help it. I was also thinking about Nina and poor young Derek. No one needed to see a dead body before the age of twenty. Of course, I wasn't sure anyone needed to see a dead body *ever.* I knew I would have been okay without it.

I was just considering pouring a cup of tea in an effort to pull myself from these morose thoughts when Owen called. I answered the phone, surprised—normally, he texted me. That, I thought, was an acknowledgment of my having mentioned how awkward I felt on the telephone most of the time. Nonetheless, I answered, happy to hear from him.

"Hello."

"Dahlia. Nina mentioned that you'd been at the spa yesterday, and I wondered if you might have some time to chat."

I was always happy to chat with Owen, and since it didn't seem likely I was going to stop thinking about the events of the past two days, I might as well discuss them with him.

"Sure," I said. "I was just about to have a cup of tea if you want to swing by the inn."

"It's not too late?"

"I wouldn't have invited you if it was."

"Okay then. I'm just around the corner. Mind if I stop by now?"

"That's perfect. I'm in the lobby."

We hung up, and a few minutes later, Owen knocked at the lobby door—which was funny since most people just walked right in.

I let him in, doing my best not to feel overwhelmed, as I often did, at how handsome he was. Sandy blond hair and bright blue eyes added to his general charm. Owen was a catch, and I often wondered what his interest was in me. But I was past the point where I was going to question it. I liked him too much for that.

We sat on the couch in front of the fireplace. "Long day?" I asked him.

"It was."

"For Nina too. She seemed so upset when I left."

Owen stared into his teacup for a moment, then looked up at me. "She was. Doesn't mean she's not a suspect, though."

That got my attention. I paused my tea halfway to my mouth. "So it *is* a murder?"

"It does look that way. We'll get the official cause of death tomorrow, but the coroner agreed that there had been some sort of blunt trauma to the head. That mark you pointed out."

I nodded, remembering the mark I'd noticed on Camille.

"Nina said Camille had been at the spa yesterday, and that you were there too. Did you happen to see anything?"

I took a sip of my tea and then set it on the table before me, taking a breath and mentally running through the events at the Paw Spa the day before. I told Owen about the various encounters I'd had—first with Camille and Lou, then with Victoria, and finally with Elliott and Emerson back here at the inn.

"And Elliott checked out before his reservation was up?" Owen asked with interest.

"He did. He said his plans had changed. That was strange, though, because he was here to judge the dog show, and that's not till this weekend."

Owen appeared to mull over this bit of information, and I was about to add more about what Nina had revealed about Victoria's tarnished reputation when the door between the lobby and the apartment burst open, and Taco and Diantha spilled out.

"Detective Sanderson!" Diantha said brightly. Taco rushed over to give Owen's hands a sound sniff and accept a few pats.

"Danny," Owen said with a broad smile. "How's school?"

I never really understood why adults always asked children how school was. Inevitably, children would answer that school was fine. It was really not a good way to learn anything about what a child was actually studying or where their interests lay, but I didn't say anything. I knew Owen was just trying to be friendly.

"It's good," my niece replied. "I was hoping I could show you guys the trick I've taught Taco."

"You've taught him one already?" I asked, looking between my niece and my dog. Taco seemed to be grinning, his tongue rolling out one side of his mouth and his eyes shining brightly as he looked at me.

"What's this?" Owen asked, leaning into my shoulder and grinning at my niece.

"Taco is going to be in the Saltcliff Dog Show," Diantha announced—though we hadn't actually entered him yet. "And I am teaching him a few tricks to help give him a better chance of winning."

"So far, she's been working on it for a couple of hours," I told Owen. "Taco must be an exceptional learner."

"Of course he is, Aunt Dolly. How else would he be able to sniff out things you shouldn't eat?" She had a point.

"Okay," Owen said, sounding almost as excited about Taco's new trick as Diantha did. "Let's see what he's got."

Diantha moved closer to where we were sitting, pushing the coffee table out of the way. "We need some room," she told us. "Come here." She looked at my dog, and he obeyed eagerly, moving to stand before her and dropping into a sit, looking up with warm caramel eyes.

"Mr. Taco," she said, and I suppressed a giggle at her haughty tone. "It is such a pleasure to meet you today." After delivering this greeting, she held out her hand as if to shake hands with Taco. He hesitated for a long moment, and something inside me flinched. It was odd—suddenly, I was very invested in whether or not this trick would be a success. I didn't want to see Diantha disappointed. I held my breath, and slowly, Taco lifted his paw. Diantha shook it eagerly, grinning the whole time and cooing at Taco. "Good boy."

Owen clapped, and I joined in. "Wow, that was awesome. That was very impressive."

"Don't worry, though. That's just the warm-up trick," Diantha told us, moving the table back into its position. "I have lots of other tricks to teach. We'll only use the most impressive ones at the dog show."

I couldn't help but admire her systematic approach.

"Well, if this one was anything to go by, he's a shoo-in," Owen said.

Diantha beamed at him, then rushed back through the apartment door, Taco on her heels.

For a moment, neither of us said anything. Then Owen took my hand and pressed it between his. Warmth flooded me, along with a little tingle of delight. I was not an affectionate person—not naturally, anyway—but I loved the affection that Owen showed me.

"She's a great kid, Dahlia." She *was*. I certainly hadn't had much to do with it, but my goal was not to undo any of the good work my sister had done in raising her. A sharp twinge of guilt crept up inside me, and I tried to push it down. I was probably getting to enjoy the best part of Diantha's life while my sister had done all the hard work.

Owen let out a heavy breath, then picked up his mug, once more wrapping his hands around it. He leaned back into the cushions of the couch, and together we watched the flames in the fireplace for a few moments. It was comfortable, being with Owen like this in silence. And that was part of what I liked most about our time together.

"So I guess that when we find the dog, we'll find the

murderer, no?" said Owen, still looking into the flames ahead of him.

I thought about that. Would someone kill Camille just to get Beau? It didn't make a lot of sense, because the murderer would not be able to show him. But I supposed, if this person was able to keep the dog hidden, they could use him as a stud. Although once again, the publicity associated with the stud's name would reveal the murderer.

I talked through these questions with Owen.

"You're right," he said. "So is it possible that two separate crimes were committed, and they were unrelated?"

I shook my head, uncertain. "I don't know. That would mean two separate motives too, right? One for stealing Beau, another for killing Camille."

"Well," said Owen, "I suppose there's still a chance that it wasn't a murder. Maybe the head wound was the result of some kind of struggle or was an accident. And I guess it's possible that Beau simply escaped."

"How do you figure that?"

Owen put his mug down and seemed to think through this idea for a moment. Then, turning to me, he said, "Well, it's a bit far-fetched, but imagine Camille had, for some reason, let herself into the spa late at night. She opened Beau's cage—maybe to pet him or just to say hello —and then somehow tripped or fell. Or maybe Beau knocked her over, and she hit her head and fell into the bath. And Beau escaped through the open door."

It was far-fetched. "First of all, why would Camille have turned on the jets in the hydrotherapy tub if she hadn't been intending to get into it?"

"Maybe she was only pretending to be wealthy? Maybe she went there to take a bath?" he suggested. I highly doubted that a woman in a Chanel suit would secretly visit a dog spa at night in order to perform her essential daily hygiene. Nor did I believe she would accidentally let her dog out the front door. That said, there was nothing to disprove it just yet.

I smiled. "I suppose it's possible."

He looked into my eyes for a moment, and I had the distinct sense that there was something he wanted to say, but he was hesitating. He pressed his lips together, dropped my gaze, then looked back up at me.

What he said was not exactly what I had been expecting. "Dahlia, I have a proposition for you."

"Proposition?" I did not know what kind of proposition Owen might have, and I wasn't about to let my brain go wild with possibilities. I waited.

"Yes. I've spoken to the chief about it already, which I hope won't bother you. But I wanted to make sure it was a possibility before I raised it with you."

My curiosity was piqued. "What is it?"

"Well, you've been so instrumental in the last couple of murders we've investigated. The chief has commented on that himself. And while I know you're not a detective, and you have no formal training, and you're not part of the police department here or anywhere, I wondered if you would be willing—or interested—in taking on a consultant role with the Saltcliff Police Department."

"Consultant?" It was an interesting idea. Of course, I had a full-time job running the inn and raising Diantha. "I don't know if I'd have time." When he didn't say anything immediately, I added, "But I *am* flattered."

"Well, I don't want to push," he said. "But it's becoming apparent that I could use your help once again. And as an official consultant, I would be able to tell you about the investigation in ways that I can't if you remain a civilian."

That was a good point. I *was* interested in solving this case. But would it be a conflict of interest, given my relationship with Owen? I raised these concerns to him, and he smiled briefly. "On paper, maybe. But Dahlia, you and I have a great relationship—working and otherwise. I don't think there would be any conflict at all, and if anything, it might bring us closer."

I guessed I just needed to consider the time commitment.

He nodded, the understanding I always saw in his gaze soothing any concerns I had about declining the offer and causing a rift between us.

"I will point out, however," Owen said with a twinkle in his eye, "that you always do seem to manage to find time to help with the investigations that have been going on since you've been here."

He had a point. "I'll definitely think about it," I told him. "Can I let you know tomorrow?"

He finished his tea, gave me a bright smile, and stood. "Of course you can."

I walked him to the door of the inn and relished the warmth of his strong arms as he pulled me in for a hug. He kissed me softly on the cheek and whispered, "Good night, Dahlia."

I watched him walk up the garden path to his car, feeling my heart beat a little faster than usual and wondering how I got so lucky.

Chapter Six

I was up early the next morning, which was not unusual, because most mornings found me in the kitchen preparing breakfast for our guests.

This morning, I was making a zucchini carrot raisin bread with a little hit of extra protein. I had read recently that women of a certain age almost certainly weren't getting enough protein, and if I could benefit from it, I figured so could my guests. It had become a new challenge for me—trying to work protein into baked goods without making them rubbery or giving them an off flavor.

Baking had always been my happy place. In a world where people's reactions and emotions did not always make sense to me, baking was a respite. Chemistry did not allow itself to be swayed by fluctuating emotions, political unrest, or teenage hormones. Instead, it relied upon exact measurements, timing, and the tiniest bit of instinct.

Occasionally, I wished I had instinct in the emotional world rather than in the kitchen, but baking was one thing I was very good at. And I supposed, since it was something people appreciated, it was a skill I was happy to have.

As I baked, I thought about Owen's offer. Of course, we had not discussed compensation, though any professional position would certainly come with some sort of remuneration. I wanted to run the idea by Amal and potentially by my friend Valerie at Beachside Bakes. Valerie had become a good friend, as we had bonded over a mutual love of baking and of Saltcliff in general. She was one of the first people I met here in Saltcliff, and she was part of what made it feel so welcoming.

Taco and I took our morning walk as soon as I had put the bread in to bake—a quick walk, as necessitated by the quick bread. I was pleased not to discover anything amiss in the neighborhood around the Saltcliff Inn this morning. When we returned, I carried the bread out to the lobby along with the scrambled egg casserole I made to go with it.

"That smells amazing," Amal said, setting her purse beneath the reception desk and lifting her nose into the air as she stood to inhale the scent.

"Zucchini carrot protein bread," I told her.

Amal's smile dropped slightly, and she raised an eyebrow. "Soon you're gonna be sneaking kale into things, aren't you?"

"Amal, you and I are both over forty. Not to put too

fine a point on it, but our bone density and muscle mass are decreasing practically by the day."

"Well, that's a thought."

"The point is, there are things we can do about it." I had satisfied myself on this matter by reading several scientific studies demonstrating that increasing protein, weight-bearing exercise, and strength training could all improve not only our health but likely our longevity. I had no intention of leaving Diantha to fend for herself. I had accepted the mantle of responsibility for raising her, and I would bear it as long as I possibly could.

"Well, it smells good at least," Amal said, eyeing the bread suspiciously.

"It tastes good too, I promise."

Amal sighed and then clicked into the reservation system for the day.

I lingered by the desk, contemplating how best to ask her advice on Owen's proposal. As usual, my hesitation was approach enough. Amal lifted her head and smiled at me. "Is there something else you would like to discuss?" she asked. "I'm up for it as long as kale is not involved."

I laughed. "No kale. There is something else, though. Last night, Owen made a proposal."

Amal's face lit up, and she actually bounced on her toes behind the desk, sending her dark hair, which was tied up in a topknot atop her head, bouncing up and down in exuberant excitement.

"He did?" She clapped her hands together. "That's amazing, Dahlia! It seems awfully sudden and maybe a bit rushed, but—oh, this is wonderful! I love a wedding!"

"Wedding?" I stared at her, unsure how she had made that leap. "What wedding?"

"Your wedding."

"I have no wedding planned. Nor is there anyone I might think of marrying anytime soon. I'm not sure what you're talking about now." I thought Amal and I understood each other well, but sometimes she still managed to confuse me.

"You said Owen proposed."

"I did not. I said he made *a* proposal last night."

Amal rolled her eyes and slumped over the desk, the energy of our supposed engagement leaving her as quickly as it had come. "Tell me about this proposal," Amal said, straightening again.

I busied my hands tidying things around the lobby while I explained what Owen had proposed. "Of course, we didn't discuss any of the details in terms of compensation or hours required," I said.

"Does any of that really matter to you?" Amal asked.

"It would be irresponsible to accept a position without fully understanding all the benefits of that position, don't you think?"

Amal chuckled, and I wasn't sure exactly what was amusing. Although that was nothing new to me. "Dahlia, you're going to say yes. You don't care about getting paid—you want to be involved in helping solve mysteries. You've done it at least three times since you got here, and I have to say, I think you really like it. And clearly, you're good at it. That's part of the reason Owen keeps coming back to you."

"Do you think he only likes me because I can help him solve mysteries?" My stomach clenched as I considered the possibility. But nothing in the evidence I'd collected suggested that Owen was using me for my mystery-solving skills.

"No, no, of course not. Owen likes you. In fact, I think Owen more than likes you. Why do you think I believed he might've proposed marriage?"

"Well, that would've been far too soon."

"Fair. But it doesn't detract from the fact that I do think Owen appreciates your ability to help him solve mysteries, and he wants to make it official."

"Yes, I think that's what he said."

Amal stared at me for a moment, as if waiting for me to say something else. And I realized, I had already made the decision.

"You're right," I said. "I think I'm going to say yes."

"Of course you are. And then you can officially help him figure out what the heck happened at the dog spa."

We had just finished this conversation when Emerson made her way to the lobby, followed by her little dog, Sir Edgar. "Good morning," she chirped brightly.

"Good morning," Amal and I both said at once.

I waved Emerson toward the breakfast items, explaining what they were. She looked them over. I didn't bother lecturing her about the importance of protein or weight-bearing exercise, figuring that whatever benefits she got could remain a secret.

"There's been some chatter on the dog show boards online," Emerson said as she sat down on the couch with a plate on her lap.

"What kind of chatter?" I didn't even know there were dog show boards.

"Well, more accusations that Victoria Dane falsified her documentation. Although I was pretty sure that scandal was put to bed already. It seems like someone's got sour grapes, dragging it up again. But of course, everyone who's ever bought a pup from Victoria has jumped in to stir the pot, worried that their investment is valueless if her stud was just some regular dog."

"Oh," I said, unsure what an appropriate answer to this would be.

Emerson went on, seemingly undaunted by my inability to keep up my end of the conversation. "And you won't believe this, but there's noise that Beaumont Royale is not going to be showing this week."

"Camille Hawthorne's Borzoi?" I clarified.

"Exactly. He was heavily favored to win Best in Show, so if he's not going to be there, that opens the playing field for other dogs." She beamed down at her little French bull-dog, who looked back up at her with something that could only be construed as love. As I watched, she slipped him a little bit of her eggs with her fingertip. "What I'm not sure about," she continued, "is why Camille would suddenly decide not to compete anymore. The woman literally lives for these things."

Emerson pulled out her phone after saying this and continued to scroll as she finished her breakfast. I didn't feel it would be appropriate to explain why I didn't think Camille was going to be competing anymore, or to point out that she literally no longer lived, so I said nothing.

We had three other rooms newly occupied by families and visitors, and as soon as everyone had been through breakfast, I cleaned up and was about to head to the police station when Owen arrived.

Chapter Seven

"Good morning," Owen said, crossing the lobby to give me a kiss on the cheek. "Hi, Amal. How are you?"

Amal had been scanning the contents of a letter she'd just opened, and she glanced up at Owen with an expression that wasn't altogether happy. She folded the letter quickly and pushed it into a pocket of her cardigan sweater. "I'm good, Owen." Amal caught my eye. "I'm going to head down and check laundry and do a supply inventory to make sure that we have everything we need for the week. I'll do the liquor inventory for the speakeasy too." She gave Owen's arm a squeeze as she passed him on her way down to the basement.

"When does the speakeasy open?" Owen asked.

"Construction was completed last week, and we received a delivery yesterday. We're still waiting on some furniture that might not be in until the end of the month. I'm hoping it'll be open by summer, but we haven't announced anything yet."

The inn made a tidy profit, and while the addition of the bar in the old speakeasy below would contribute, there was a lot more to learn about running that operation before I was comfortable launching it. Plus, staff to hire and the liquor license to obtain.

"Makes sense," Owen said, leaning his forearms over the front of the reception desk. "Sorry to just pop in, but I wondered if you'd considered my proposal any further. And if you happen to be planning to say yes, I have some-thing to show you."

I loved the way Owen always made room for me to be myself—he knew I was going to say yes, but he wasn't going to be pushy.

"I *am* planning to say yes," I said, looking into his deep blue eyes. "I mean, yes. I do say yes. As long as it won't be... odd. Us working together."

Owen's smile didn't fade as we walked back to the couch where we'd sat the night before. "It won't be odd unless we make it that way, Dahlia."

Maybe he was right. I sat down next to him. "Okay, then. What's first?"

"I have the autopsy report here. I thought we could review it together."

"You haven't looked at it yet?" I glanced at the folder in his hands.

"I might've given it a quick peek," he admitted. "But I haven't processed every detail."

"Tell me what it says then," I suggested.

Owen opened the folder, and I kept my eyes off the photos of poor Camille Hawthorne laid out on a table. She wasn't an especially pleasant person, but that didn't change the fact that I was sad to see her killed.

"The determination is that Camille died by drowning sometime in the early hours of the morning. She hadn't been dead long when the body was discovered. Maybe a couple hours," Owen said. "But the head wound was sustained earlier. Potentially hours before she drowned."

I frowned, meeting Owen's eyes. "So she didn't hit her head falling into the tub and then drown?"

He shook his head. "Doesn't look like it. Seems like she sustained a pretty serious head wound first and then somehow ended up in the tub later."

"Well, that gives us more questions than answers," I said. "For one thing, why was Camille back at the Paw Spa that night? Beau had been boarded, and she should have been happy to leave him there until morning, one would think."

"One would think," Owen agreed.

"And then, question two, who else was in the Paw Spa

after hours? Do they have any security cameras or anything?"

"Good thinking," Owen said. "They do. Only on the front door—it doesn't show any of the interior unfortunately, but we're gathering the footage from that night now. We should have it soon."

I nodded, thinking. "Well, that will be it, won't it? Whoever the footage shows arriving after hours besides Camille would be our dognapping killer."

Owen blew out a short breath. "It's rarely that simple, but I hope you're right."

"The other question is, how did Camille even get inside after hours? Did she have a key?"

"The door locks with a code," Owen said. "And Nina is supposed to be getting us a list of everyone with the code."

That made sense. That should tell us most of what we needed to know.

"There was also a lot of dark dog fur found on Camille's coat."

"Her dog is white," I remembered.

"So that could be a clue... though the whole place caters to dogs, so having fur floating around isn't exactly unusual."

"True. Maybe she took the coat off and dropped it on the floor?"

"Or maybe Camille was on the floor at some point."

I tried to imagine Camille Hawthorne voluntarily lying

on the spa floor. "I doubt that. It seems like Nina might be of some help at this point. Should we go visit her now?" I asked.

Owen grinned at me. "Definitely. But I have a couple of things for you to sign first, from the captain. This will make your consultancy official." He walked me through the contract for my consulting services and the rate of payment the Saltcliff Police Department proposed, which I thought was reasonable. Once all the paperwork was finished, I went down to let Amal know I was going to step out.

"Amal?" I stepped through the door between the basement and the speakeasy, taking in the shining copper ceiling and the gleaming wood bar. The place was coming together and I felt a twinge of pride looking at it.

"Yes?" Amal popped up from behind the big bar where we'd stored most of the inventory delivery. Her usually placid face carried a worried expression.

"Are you all right?" I wasn't used to seeing Amal looking less than serene.

"I am," she said in an unconvincing tone. "I've just had a bit of news from home, is all. It's on my mind."

"Nothing bad, I hope."

"It will be okay," she said, waving a hand as if to dismiss the topic completely. It was clear she didn't want to talk about it, so I let it go. For now.

"I wanted to let you know that Owen and I are going

over to the Paw Spa to chat with Nina Reyes for a bit. Taco and Danny are in the apartment."

"Still working on tricks?" Amal asked with a smile.

"Yes. Taco is really being put through his paces. He can shake, roll over, and beg. I'm not sure if that last one is a great idea, though. He already has enough trouble containing himself around food."

"The drooling?" Amal asked.

"Yes, exactly." Poor Taco. His appointed profession was to sniff my food for me, but food was the one thing he really, really loved. To sniff food without eating it? Well, it just showed how dedicated and wonderful my service dog really was.

"Okay," Amal said. "I'll head back up in just a second in case anyone needs anything. This can wait."

"Thanks, Amal."

I turned and walked with Owen to the Paw Spa, where Nina Reyes was chatting with a customer at the front desk. When we walked through the door, her eyebrows rose, and she stumbled momentarily on her words. "That's... that's... yes, that's fine. Thanks, Ms. Damlin."

Nina busied herself with a stack of mail behind the desk as a familiar face turned toward the door, shifting into a smile when she saw me. "Dahlia, hello, neighbor! Why has it been so long since I've given you a reading?" Tessa Damlin lived next door to the inn, and she thought of herself as something of a psychic. I, however, remained a skeptic.

Her gaze slid to Owen. "And I see you are out and about on the arm of your handsome beau."

I felt the heat in my cheeks. This was part of what I'd been worried about. We were on official police business! But Owen was my boyfriend. Of course, it was going to confuse people.

Before I could say a word, Owen spoke up. "Dahlia here is actually acting in an official capacity today. She's joined the force."

Tessa's mouth dropped open. "You're giving up inn-keeping for police work? Where is your gun?" She gave me an up-and-down gaze.

"I'm just a consultant," I said quickly. "And it is good to see you, Tessa. Let's have tea soon."

"If by tea you mean moonshine, then I'm all in," she said, laughing. "Be good, lovebirds."

My blush deepened as humiliation threatened to swamp me. "I'm so sorry," I whispered to Owen, but he gave me a bright smile.

"Why? She's hilarious." She was, actually. And Owen didn't seem to mind her teasing.

"Detective. Dahlia. Can I help you with something?" Nina looked around quickly, as if we were in the way. "I was cleared to reopen. I have the notice here somewhere."

"Of course," Owen said. "Everything is good. We just hoped we might ask a couple of questions about Camille Hawthorne."

"Here? Now?" Nina gazed around the busy spa once again.

"If you don't mind," Owen said. "Or we could go down to the station if you prefer." His tone made it clear we'd be speaking one way or another.

Nina wrung her hands. "I only have a few minutes—another dog show contestant is coming in for a hydrotherapy session. We can go in here." She took us into the back, where the dog kennels for boarding dogs were. The kennels were all empty at the moment.

"Perfect," Owen said. He pulled out his phone. "I'm going to record, okay?"

"Sure." Nina was glancing repeatedly at me, as if curious why I was here.

"I'm working with the detective now," I said, hoping to explain.

Nina nodded.

"Nina, can you tell us if Camille Hawthorne had the code to the front door of the spa?" Owen held his phone at his side, and I realized that probably allowed people to forget about the recording, put them more at ease.

"She did, yes. A few VIP customers who boarded here from time to time had the code. I'm getting that list together for the police," she reminded us.

"Right, sure. Do you remember, just off the top of your head, who else might be on that list?"

Nina looked around, as if searching for the answer. "Let's see. The employees, of course—Derek and me. And then a few VIPs like Camille—Victoria Dane, Simone Jeffries, Ronald Antonian..." She trailed off, her eyes looking up toward the ceiling. "There are a few others, but I still haven't had a chance to dig into my records to get them all listed."

Owen nodded. "Can you get us contact information for those few you mentioned?"

"Sure. I can just pull up an invoice for each—that'll have all their info on it."

"That works." Owen nodded. He glanced around the kennel space once more. "Can you show us where Beau was being kept the night he disappeared?"

Nina nodded and moved to the first big kennel along the wall. There were three total, each like a small room containing a cot, a food and water bowl, and a few toys. The walls were made of dark wood between the kennels, and the fronts were close-linked fence material with doors built in. I figured this allowed keepers to see inside the kennels, but the dogs couldn't see one another.

"He was in here," she said, her gaze dropping. "I just can't imagine who would steal a dog."

I couldn't either. My mind flashed to Taco, and I was glad he was safe at home with Diantha. I stepped nearer to the kennel, peering inside, then looked left and right around the room where the kennels were. There was something I hadn't noticed before at the back of the room.

"Nina, where does that door lead?" I pointed out a heavy door with a deadbolt on it.

"That goes to the alley behind the shop."

Owen and I exchanged a glance. "Was it locked the morning you discovered Beau missing?" Owen asked.

"We always keep it locked," Nina said. "But I don't... I don't really know. There was so much going on that morning."

So whoever took Beau could have left through this back door.

"Do you have a camera on the back door?" Owen asked.

Nina shook her head.

When we were finished in the back, we headed to the front again, and Nina printed out the invoices and handed them to Owen. We said goodbye to her and headed back outside.

"Wanna grab a seat?" Owen gestured to the bench near the door of the Paw Spa. "We can go through these quickly and figure out next steps."

"Sure." I sat at his side, momentarily distracted by the cool spring breeze blowing down the sidewalk and the way the eucalyptus trees hung down to shade the street.

"Okay," Owen said, shuffling through the papers. "Oh,

well, this is kind of interesting." He handed me one of the pages. "Camille's invoice is marked unpaid."

"Maybe it's recent and she just hadn't paid yet?"

"Look at the date. This is from last fall." We exchanged a look. Camille was running around town with a luxury pet, wearing Chanel suits, and carrying purses that probably cost more than the Fiat I drove. "Was Camille struggling to pay?"

"Do you really think Camille had money problems?" I couldn't imagine it.

"It seems like it," Owen said. "Maybe Nina was letting her slide, just being kind."

"Maybe," I said, feeling a twinge of guilt for the assumptions I'd made about Camille. Maybe she really had come back to the Paw Spa just to take a bath. Poor woman.

"Well, we can ask Nina about that. For now, I'll call the rest of these folks and have them come down for questioning."

"Okay. What should I do?" I asked.

"I'll get in touch when we have the surveillance footage. Maybe we can pursue the dognapping case from there."

"Sounds good."

Owen and I rose and said goodbye. From there, we went our separate ways—me to the inn, Owen back to the station.

Amal was nowhere to be found when I arrived back at the inn, which was fine because Diantha and Taco were in the lobby should anyone need anything.

"There you are," Diantha said.

I looked around, a bit confused. I hadn't been hiding. "Yes, here I am. Have you been looking for me?"

She shrugged and kicked one foot in a way I found charming for some reason. "Not looking for you. Just... missing you, I guess."

A spark of warmth bloomed in my chest as I took in my niece's apple-round cheeks and bright dark eyes. She looked so much like Daisy sometimes it was hard to believe my sister was really gone. "Well, what's going on?"

"Only that I have another trick to show you. Taco is brilliant, you know."

I knew that Taco was brilliant. I was glad that other people appreciated it too. I just wasn't sure he was going to win a dog show where dogs worth thousands and thousands of dollars would be competing on their looks.

"Watch this," Diantha said. She moved to where Taco was curled in a ball on his bed and used her most excited voice to rouse him. "Come on, Taco."

Taco jumped up eagerly, probably believing he was about to be fed. Diantha pulled something from her pocket, which appeared to be a scarf that had been hanging in my closet—one of Daisy's. She held it out to Taco.

"Scent, scent."

Then she looked at me. "Okay, you keep Taco here for a minute."

With these odd words, she disappeared down the main hallway, past the door to the basement, where I couldn't see her anymore. A few moments later, she returned without the scarf. She went back to Taco, who was still sitting, waiting for her command, and patted his head.

"Taco, okay, find it." Taco launched into action, his nose to the ground like some kind of scent hound, sniffing along the trail that Diantha had followed down the hall. We went with him, and I was amused as he stopped and sniffed excitedly around an outlet on the wall.

Diantha whispered to me, "I rubbed the scarf there. See how smart he is?"

Taco continued sniffing, then seemed to pick up something else a little farther down the hall. He dashed ahead, took a moment to look around, then proceeded to the very end of the hall where there was a potted plant beneath the window. He sniffed around the plant until he seemed to decide something, then sat and barked once.

Diantha hurried down the hall after him. Taco's expectant gaze stayed fixed on her as she reached behind the potted plant and fished out the scarf. "Good dog. Good boy."

She pulled a treat from her pocket and gave it to Taco.

"That was very impressive, Danny," I said.

"I know, right? He's practically a detective just like you."

That got me thinking. "You know what?" I asked, my brain whirling. I looked at her excitedly, and Taco's eyes were on me. They both stared at me while I finished processing my thought. "How would you guys like to help solve a little mystery?" I did not want to involve Diantha in the murder aspect of Camille Hawthorne's situation, but I wondered if Taco and Diantha could be of help in locating Beau. I explained the dognapping situation and asked Diantha what she thought. "Beau's collar was left behind," I told her. "Do you think that would be enough for Taco to get his scent?"

My niece looked at Taco for a moment, as if assessing his capabilities visually, and then nodded. "I think so. He has a very sensitive sniffer."

"He does, you're right."

"It's worth a try, Aunt Dolly."

I returned to the lobby, where I texted Owen this idea. He agreed it was worth a try and said he'd call Nina and ask her to give us the collar. It had not been taken as evidence, but Nina had been asked to hold it in case it became a clue. Diantha and I agreed to go pick up the collar and let Taco do his job as soon as I got some of the baking handled for the following days. I needed a little break from detective work anyway, and baking always soothed me. We returned to the lobby just as Amal was coming back up from the basement.

"Oh, you're back," she said.

"I am. Danny and I are going to run over to the Paw Spa for a bit with Taco to chase down a lead." I looked at her a bit more closely. Were Amal's eyes red? Had my friend been crying? "Are you all right?"

Taco had rushed ahead into the lobby with Diantha, and I paused in the hallway. Amal's dark eyes searched my face, and I sensed she was about to say something, but she seemed to change her mind and dropped my gaze. "It's fine. Nothing—it'll work itself out."

"If you say so, but if you need anything..." I wasn't sure how to offer my friend support because I didn't know what was wrong.

She grasped my arm for a moment, as if to steady herself. "Thank you." With that, she dropped her hand and headed back toward the lobby, where she began straightening up pillows on the couch, stoking the fire, and collecting discarded cups and plates from around the room.

"Will you be OK if we're gone for a bit?"

"Of course," she said, smiling at me, and I realized that whatever was bothering Amal would likely remain a secret. She would tell me when and if it became necessary. Our hotel manager was my best friend, but she was also an extremely private person, and as I entered the apartment through the adjoining door, I realized there was much about Amal Kapoor that I did not know.

Chapter Eight

Diantha, Taco, and I walked over to the Paw Spa to meet Nina and retrieve Beau's collar. Nina was at the door when we arrived, looking every bit as nervous as she had the last few times I'd seen her. I assumed between the murder and the impending dog show, she was under quite a lot of stress. Who could blame her?

"Here's the collar," Nina said, holding out a plastic bag into which I assumed the investigators had placed it. "How do you think it will help you find Beau?"

Diantha was practically giddy with excitement, and Taco was picking up every bit of her enthusiasm, whining gently as he sensed his role was approaching.

"I'm not sure it will," I admitted. "But Danny has a theory. You're welcome to watch."

"Do you mind if we come inside for a little bit?" Diantha asked.

"That's fine, I've just closed up." Nina ushered us in, where the spa was silent, closed for the evening. Diantha walked Taco to the middle of the room and had him sit. Then she put the collar close to his face and directed him to scent.

Taco eagerly sniffed the collar, and for a moment, I wondered if he recognized the scent of the friend he'd encountered so briefly on the sidewalk.

"Find!" Diantha pointed toward the floor of the spa, and Taco stood and dropped his head, following directions like the excellent boy he was.

"Your dog is going to find Beau?" Nina did not sound very convinced that Taco would be able to accomplish this task, but I was rooting for my dog. And, of course, for Beau, who I hoped hadn't come to any harm through all this.

Taco scented eagerly all around the interior of the Paw Spa, but he didn't seem overly enthusiastic about any one spot, nor did he sit and alert as he had done in the hallway before. He nosed around the grooming room, and the base of the hydrotherapy tub, where he paused and whined. I moved closer to where he was pressing his nose to the base of the tub and spotted something that had been pushed almost under the tub.

"Do you have a pen?" I asked Nina.

"Sure," she said, moving to the desk and returning with a pen, which she handed to me.

I pushed the end of the pen under the tub behind the object and was able to pull it out. It was gold in color, and a little scratched up, but appeared to be a link from a chain. "What's this?" I asked, holding it out for Nina to see.

She laughed. "You should see the leashes and collars people bring their dogs in with. It looks like a link from a gold collar."

I could definitely picture it, after having seen Camille's diamond-studded collar for Beaumont Royale. I handed the link to Nina, and she dropped it into a drawer behind the desk.

Taco returned to Diantha, and she tried once more, letting him sniff the collar and then sending him off to scent.

This time, he paused at the door to the back room where the kennels were. When I stepped forward and opened it for him, he rushed inside eagerly, sniffing the kennel where Beau had stayed.

"He really does smell Beau," Nina said wonderingly.

Taco actually entered the kennel and then came back out, whining slightly as he continued pressing his nose to the ground and wagging his tail eagerly. He followed the line of the kennels and disappeared around the last one, heading straight to the back door of the Paw Spa, where he sat and alerted.

"He found something," I said eagerly, rushing to the spot where Taco sat.

"He found the back door," Nina said, her wonder at Taco's skill clearly dissipating.

"Is it possible that Beau went out this door?" I asked her.

"Well, if I was going to take a dog from the kennels, I'd probably take them out the back," she said. "There's only a camera on the front door."

That did make sense. "Maybe we open the door?"

Nina nodded and struggled with the deadbolt.

"Is the lock not working?" I asked.

"It's been a little weird lately," she said.

Finally, she managed to turn it, and the door swung open into an alleyway that did not meet most people's definitions of an alley. There were no dumpsters, no sinister-looking stray cats, or dark figures lurking about. Instead, the alley was cobbled and filled with potted plants, blooming flowers, and quaint balconies hanging off the backs of buildings. Just outside the Paw Spa, there was a tiny cocktail table and two chairs with a flowering gardenia set atop it. I had no idea some alleys in Saltcliff were every bit as charming as the rest of the town. Atop the table was an ashtray and several half-smoked cigarette butts.

"This is adorable," I said, looking around.

Nina glanced at me and smiled. "When it's quiet, I often eat lunch out here." I nodded. I could imagine eating my lunch here on a quiet afternoon, watching the birds visit the many window boxes overhead.

"This is a great place to eat. Or smoke," I suggested.

Nina's mouth dropped open. "I don't smoke." Then she followed my gaze to the table. "Oh, that was an old friend in town for the dog show. We sat out here when he first arrived in town, and he smoked a bit."

I nodded my understanding and gave the adorable alley one more appreciative gaze. Taco, however, was not nearly as charmed by the alleyway. He was busy. He was already halfway down the alley, sniffing furiously, and my niece was just behind him, holding the end of his leash.

"I think we're headed off, Nina," I called over my shoulder. "Thank you for staying and opening the spa for us."

She watched us go, lifting a hand in farewell as I jogged to catch up with Diantha and Taco.

Taco led us down the alley and then turned out onto Clove Street, glancing around himself only for a second before returning his nose to the ground. Whatever he smelled, he seemed very certain he was on the right path.

"Danny, I have to say, I'm impressed. I had no idea Taco could follow a scent like this."

Diantha grinned up at me, her arm out ahead of her as she allowed Taco to lead the way. He sniffed along the sidewalk outside a row of small cottages, pausing here and there and then returning determinedly to his route. Part of me wondered if perhaps he smelled a treat or was just chasing a squirrel, but I didn't want to say that out loud. Instead, I followed along his chosen route willingly, only a tiny bit surprised when he drew up outside the Regal Retreat, an upscale kennel facility near the Saltcliff School.

"The Regal Retreat?" Diantha looked between me and the building before us excitedly. "It's a dog kennel! Do you think Beau is here?"

I shrugged. If he was, he had certainly not made the choice to switch accommodations of his own accord. "I guess Taco thinks he is," I said. Taco had dropped to a sit and let out one bark outside the front gate of the building, which looked like a long low cottage. The bark was answered by several others. We followed the sounds around the side of the building, to a small door along a fence running the length of the business in the back alley. There was a door set into the fence with a small window at the top. Diantha and Taco weren't tall enough to peer through, but I did—and it appeared the visiting dogs were enjoying some outdoor time in the small yard behind the building.

And there, in the midst of the golden retrievers and poodles owned by regular Saltcliff citizens, was Beaumont Royale, Camille Hawthorne's prized Borzoi. He appeared utterly unharmed and actually seemed to be having a lovely time playing with all the other dogs.

I turned to Diantha and Taco, who waited patiently behind me. "You did it! Beau is in there playing!"

"He is?" Diantha gasped. "Lift me up so I can see?" I did as she asked, hoisting her slender frame up by the hips so she could peer through the window. "Oh, Beau! You're safe," she cried.

I slid her back to the ground and pulled out my phone. "I'll let Owen know he's here."

"Aren't we going to go in and rescue him?" Diantha asked.

I gazed at Beau again, and then back to my niece. "No, I think now that we know he's safe, we better get Owen involved first."

"Well, we're here and we have Taco... maybe we could pretend to be scoping out a boarding option for him? Get a look inside?" Diantha seemed to have adapted quickly to her role as investigator. "It'll be like being undercover, Aunt Dolly!"

I considered this, and as I was about to say I didn't think it was a good idea, Owen texted me back that he was on his way. He asked us not to leave, just in case Beau somehow got moved in the meantime.

"Okay," I said. "I guess we can go in."

We walked back around to the front and knocked at the door, which was immediately opened by a tall thin woman with dark green-framed glasses perched on a long slim nose. "Can I help you?"

"Hello," I said, realizing it was actually quite late to be visiting a business. "I, uh, so sorry to bother you..."

"We're hoping to take a quick look around to see if maybe Taco might board with you when we go on our big trip to Denmark," Diantha said brightly.

My mouth dropped open. "Denmark?"

The woman didn't seem to notice anything amiss, since she waved us inside and took a moment to lavish Taco with a bit of love. "Denmark is beautiful," she said. "What time of year are you thinking of going?"

"Soon," Diantha said. We exchanged a quiet look. I was amazed how easily the lies seemed to come to her. Perhaps that wasn't a good thing...

"Well, we're quite booked, usually several months ahead with a one or two-night spot here and there. But I'm happy to show you around, either way. I'm Marla Carver, owner of the Regal Retreat."

"Nice to meet you," I said, beginning to feel more comfortable in my role as future traveler to Denmark. "I'm Dahlia and this is my niece, Diantha."

"Everyone calls me Danny," Diantha corrected quickly.

Marla led us through the lobby and into a long hallway with doors on either side. Each door had a pane of glass down it, with a curtain on the outside that could be pulled over the glass.

"As you can see, all our accommodations are luxury dog suites, with a bed, television, and rug."

"The dogs get TVs?" Diantha asked, amazed.

Marla smiled. "They do, but we don't always put them on. Some dogs are used to their owners leaving the television on when they're away to keep them company." Diantha and Taco exchanged a wide-eyed look, as if considering whether he might need this luxury.

"Each suite comes with a daily doggy ice cream treat, three playtimes in the yard out back, and a daily one-on-one petting session if requested. All dogs are washed and dried once during their stay."

We walked along the line of doors, and at the last one, Taco sat and barked once. This must be where Beau was staying.

Marla gave him a quizzical look but then smiled. "It's okay, Taco." She patted his head and walked us to the enclosure out back where the dogs were running around and playing. "My daughter Sophie is supervising playtime right now," she said, indicating the girl standing in the center of the play yard. She was a young woman, maybe twenty years old, and could have been Marla's double, except she was about a foot shorter. "We like to be sure everyone gets along."

"It seems very nice," I said, just as a loud "dong" rang out.

"Oh my, that's someone else at the front door," she said, glancing at us with wide eyes. "It's a busy night!"

I didn't want to tell her that I'd called the police. It wouldn't come off well, and she would find out soon enough. As expected, when we went back to the front and Marla opened the door, Owen was there with two other officers behind him. "Marla Carver?" he said, his friendly smile never wavering.

"Yes?" Marla's voice shook. "Is something wrong?"

"Maybe," Owen said. "Mind if we come inside?"

Marla stepped back, glancing between me and Owen with a deep furrow between her eyebrows. "What's going on?"

"Is he still here?" Owen asked me.

I nodded, and Marla's eyes narrowed at me. "You're not really here to look at boarding your dog, are you?"

"Not right now," I admitted. "Though your facilities are lovely."

Marla sniffed and turned back to Owen.

"We have reason to believe a very valuable missing show dog is being housed here," he said. "Are you familiar with Beaumont Royale, the Borzoi belonging to Camille Hawthorne?" Owen held out a photo on his phone.

Marla shrugged and shook her head. "We have a Borzoi here at the moment, but his name isn't Beaumont Royale. It's Sam."

"Sam?" Diantha said, laughing. I elbowed her lightly to

suggest maybe interfering in Owen's interview wasn't a good idea.

"Who is Sam's owner?" Owen asked.

"Well, we can just check and see who registered him here," she said. Marla's unease seemed to have turned to annoyance as she moved to the computer screen and began furiously typing at the keyboard. "Here. He was brought in by his owner. Lou Grant."

Diantha and I exchanged a look. Lou Grant was the name of the man we'd met outside the Paw Spa that first day—the handler Camille had just fired. I didn't mention this for the moment, wondering if Lou had dognapped Beau to get back at Camille.

While Owen questioned Marla, the other officers went into the back of the facility, obviously looking for Beau. "He's out back with all the dogs, playing," Diantha said helpfully.

"Is Lou Grant a regular customer of the Regal Retreat?" Owen asked Marla.

She shook her head. "No, I don't really know him at all. He made a last-minute reservation for Sam and brought him in the same night."

"And when was that?" Owen asked.

"Two or three days ago," Marla said. "I don't remember exactly. We're always so busy, it was surprising I even had a space for him."

"And when is Lou scheduled to come back to pick Sam up?"

Marla peered at the computer screen, frowning as she pushed her glasses back up her nose. "It looks like tomorrow," she said, but the words came out like a question.

"And I assume you have a phone number for this Lou Grant?" Owen asked, coming around the desk to look at the reservation.

Marla shifted her weight and let out a few nervous sounds as she grabbed the mouse and moved it around quickly. "I was in such a hurry, I didn't... I didn't even put his number on this. But of course, I have it somewhere."

"If you could just write it down for me when you find it, that would be great."

Owen smiled at Marla as if this was just another day and not a big deal. Then he looked at me, his eyes narrowing ever so slightly—telling me he thought we were onto something. If nothing else, I was happy to have found Beau unharmed. Although, I supposed there was a small chance Sam wasn't actually Beau.

One of the officers returned to the lobby and addressed Owen. "The girl out there won't let us take the dog."

Marla looked up from the computer screen. "That's because Sophie is very protective of our boarders."

"Well, I think maybe we should leave Sam here tonight anyway," Owen said, to my surprise. "Marla obviously takes very good care of the dogs she boards, and I'm sure nothing would happen to him here. And he'll certainly be much more comfortable here than at the police station."

Marla had no choice but to agree.

"And in the morning, we'll give you a call and come back to see Sam."

"Okay, if that's what you think is best. Should I call Lou?" Marla asked.

"No, I don't think you should," Owen said. "Let's let him finish enjoying whatever trip he might be on, and we'll have a chat with him tomorrow. I'm sure he would hate to be disturbed, and the last thing we want to do is get him worrying about his beloved dog... Sam."

A few moments later, we were all leaving the Regal Retreat, as a very nervous-looking Marla watched us go. The two officers headed to a squad car, and Owen suggested they go ahead and that he would see them the next day. "Walk you home?" Owen asked, looking between Diantha and me.

I nodded and said, "Sure."

Taco trotted happily as we left, seeming to understand that his duty had been done. As we walked, Owen and I chatted.

"So you actually think that is a dog named Sam?" I asked him.

"Not even a little bit," Owen said. "But I do think that he's in better hands there than he would be at the police station. And if she wanted to hurt him, she would've done it already."

"So you think Marla is the dognapper?" I asked, voicing the question in my own mind.

"Well, we certainly can't be sure, can we? We need to talk to her a little bit more and track down Lou Grant." I had already told Owen about Camille's former dog handler and that he had seemed to be departing under dark circumstances when I'd seen him the other day.

"If Lou Grant really does have Beau, that would be a coincidence, wouldn't it?" Diantha asked. "Since he was Camille's handler?"

Owen and I agreed.

"But what we really need is to figure out if there's any kind of identifying mark or characteristic that will help us know definitively whether this dog is Beaumont Royale," Diantha said.

I hadn't thought about that. I had assumed there just weren't very many Borzois around and that this one had to be Beau. But with the dog show in town, that probably wasn't a safe assumption.

"Beaumont Royale has a pretty lengthy, well-developed web presence," Diantha said.

I looked at her. "How do you know that?"

"I've been sniffing out the competition for a while."

That actually did make sense.

"We can look back through his online photos and see if

we find anything that would be definitively identifying," she told Owen. "We'll let you know what we find tomorrow."

"I'm guessing he might be microchipped too," Owen said quietly to me, and I realized he wanted to let Diantha help if she wanted to and didn't want to dash her hopes with this bit of information.

We were just turning the corner toward the inn when Owen smiled at me and laced his fingers through mine. "See? This working together thing is working out well, right?"

"Maybe it is," I said.

"Have you found a dress for the policeman's ball?"

"Not yet," I told him, butterflies springing to life once again inside me as I considered an overnight stay in the city with Owen.

He walked us to the front door of the inn, held it open for us, and then kissed me on the cheek. "I'll give you a call first thing tomorrow," he said. "I'm assuming you'll want to be around for the questioning when we find Lou."

"Wouldn't miss it."

The following morning, I put out a spread of lemon poppyseed muffins I'd made the day before, along with rashers of thick bacon and a plate of scrambled eggs. The inn was beginning to fill up in anticipation of the dog show this coming weekend.

Taco was more excited than ever at the number of pets staying with us at the Saltcliff B&B. In addition to Emerson's French bulldog, there were now two German shepherds, a giant schnauzer, a tiny Chihuahua who spent most of his time being carried in a very fancy bag, and an enormous mixed-breed dog that I had been told, alternately, was a very expensive French hybrid or a rescue from San Francisco. Either way, we weren't snooty about our dogs at the Saltcliff B&B, and it was a joy to see so many four-legged friends rolling around the back lawn, sniffing through the garden, and sitting quietly at their owners' feet as people gathered in the lobby for meals and evening companionship.

It was the middle of spring break, and Diantha had spent most of her time ensuring that learning was not overlooked. Of course, it was *Taco's* learning she was most concerned with, not her own. However, she did find the necessary paperwork to register Taco in the weekend's dog show activities.

"There's a skills category, and there's an all-around best dog category," she said excitedly.

I had learned from a few of the dog show enthusiasts in

town that even the fanciest dog shows—at least in our area —tended to include categories for amateur canines and their handlers.

"Well, those both sound appropriate. Can you enter in both?" I asked my niece.

Her eyes glowed, and she clutched the papers tightly enough to wrinkle the edges. "I was hoping you would say that. I didn't want to ask for too much."

I smiled excitedly, and I surprised myself by leaning in and giving her a quick hug. Normally, hugs were something I planned a bit or thought about well in advance. It was very possible that this was the first time in my life I had ever spontaneously hugged anyone.

I was proud of the way Diantha and I were both growing up.

Chapter Nine

Owen and I had arranged to meet at the police station, where both Marla and Lou had agreed to come in for questioning. It was an odd sensation approaching the officer at the desk and telling him who I was. He smiled graciously and reached into a drawer at his side, extracting an ID card with my name on it.

"When you come in from now on, you can badge in over here," he said, walking me to the turnstile at the side of the desk.

It felt so official. Of course, I didn't get a badge, or a gun, or even an office, but I *could* badge myself through a turnstile in the lobby. He still had to hit a button that unlocked the door into the interrogation area for me, but I felt like I'd come up in the world, nonetheless.

"You can head into the back," he said. "Owen is expecting you. Interrogation room one."

With that, he hit the buzzer on the door, and I entered the sterile, cold hallway at the back of the station. The interrogation rooms were on the left, and I headed through the door into the first one. Owen met me in the small vestibule outside the interrogation room, where a one-way mirror allowed me to see Lou Grant sitting at the table inside.

"Hey," Owen said.

I greeted him, my eyes on Lou, who did not look happy at all.

"Should we get started?" Owen asked, nodding toward the door. "Seems like he has a lot of other things to do today."

"Sure," I said. I had a list of questions on my phone—one for Lou and one for Marla. But as we walked through the door and Lou's angry gaze fell upon me, I found I was more than happy to let Owen do the talking.

"Mr. Grant, I think you've met Dahlia Vale before."

"Chocolate Lab. English. Weird name. I never forget a dog." Lou turned back to Owen after barking these words at me. Owen and I both took a seat across from him.

"Mr. Grant, thank you for coming in today. We wanted to chat with you about a very valuable show dog who was recently taken from a boarding kennel at the Paw Spa."

"Go on." Lou frowned at us, his eyes narrowing to slits. He leaned back in his chair and crossed his arms, clearly not enjoying the direction this was going.

"Yes, the dog in question is a Borzoi, owned by Camille Hawthorne. His name was Beaumont Royale."

"I know of him."

"That's right, you were Beau's handler for a while, weren't you?" Owen asked.

"I was."

Owen's voice remained friendly, his attitude easy and approachable. "And do you handle any other Borzois, Mr. Grant?"

"Nope. He was the only one I ever handled. Pretty rare dog."

"So do you *have* a Borzoi?" Owen asked him.

Mr. Grant shook his head, uncrossing his arms and balling his fists on top of the table. He leaned forward as he spoke. "No. What is this about?"

"Good question. The owner of the Regal Retreat identified you as the person who checked in a Borzoi matching Beaumont Royale's description a few days ago." Mr. Grant began to sputter, his face turning bright red. Owen went on. "Did you check in a Borzoi, Mr. Grant?"

"How could I check in a dog I don't have? I don't understand how this is getting pointed at me. I don't even know where the Regal Retreat is."

Owen waited for Mr. Grant to settle a bit, and when his knuckles had regained their usual color, he continued. "No one is accusing you of anything, Mr. Grant. We're merely trying to get to the bottom of this dognapping case."

"Well, I *didn't* take Beaumont Royale, and I *didn't* check him into the Regal Retreat. I've had nothing to do with that dog or his horrible owner since the day I saw *you* at the Paw Spa." He pointed one meaty finger at me as he spat this last bit.

"Mr. Grant, do you think you would be able to identify Beaumont Royale?"

"Of course I would. I handled that dog for several years. I know his every mannerism, his every foible."

I felt my eyebrows go up at the thought. Dogs had *foibles?*

Owen picked up his phone, scrolling a couple of times before finally pulling up a video to show Mr. Grant. "This is the dog that was checked into the Regal Retreat. In your professional opinion, is this dog Beaumont Royale?"

Mr. Grant watched the Borzoi romp with the other dogs in the play yard at the Regal Retreat on Owen's phone. After a moment, he nodded with conviction. "That's him."

"How can you be so sure?" I asked, curiosity getting the better of me.

"When he runs, you see the way he picks up his front feet? It was something we worked on when he was a puppy." I watched the dog in the footage run, and he did *prance* in a way the other dogs did not.

"Is that a trait specific to Borzois?" I asked, my curiosity piqued.

"No. It was a Camille Hawthorne thing. She wanted Beau to be special. And she wanted him to be noticed. But I can also tell it's him by the set of his ears. Each dog is a little different that way. And see how he keeps moving to where the Cocker Spaniel is? Beau was always fond of Cockers for whatever reason."

"So you're saying there's no question in your mind that this dog is Beaumont Royale?" Owen asked Mr. Grant.

"I'd bet my life on it."

"And you absolutely did not check this dog into the Regal Retreat under the name Sam?"

That made Lou Grant laugh. "If I was going to dognap a prize-winning show dog, why would I check him into a kennel? He would surely be identified."

"That's pretty much what we thought," Owen told him, nodding.

"So let me get this straight—you're telling me someone else checked this dog into this kennel using *my* name?"

"Looks like it," Owen said.

Lou Grant's face began to redden again. Clearly, he did not like someone framing him.

"Do you by chance know a Marla Carver?" Owen asked.

Lou's lips pressed firmly shut. After glancing at both of us, he let out a sigh. "Might have dated her a few times. A long time ago."

Owen and I exchanged a glance. "How did that end?" Owen asked.

"Not very well," Lou said. "She's a bit of a nutter. Had to break things off."

"How did she take that?" Owen asked.

Lou shook his head. "Well, she wasn't happy about it."

"How long ago was that, Mr. Grant?" I asked.

"Years," he said.

If Marla had chosen his name out of spite, she sure could hold a grudge, I thought.

"How did you and Marla meet?" I asked.

"The dog world is a small one. She was handling a dog in the toy category when I met Camille. We had a lot in common."

"And when is the last time you saw her?" Owen asked.

"She left the circuit a few years back. After we, uh... broke up."

"One more question," Owen said. "Do you know of anyone who might have been looking to steal Camille Hawthorne's dog?"

Lou whistled low and long, letting his head shake slowly side to side. "Well, I can tell you this—that woman had more enemies than friends. But you don't steal a dog like Beau unless you're desperate for some reason. You can't show him, you can't sell him, and you can't use him for a stud. He's so well-known, he'd basically be worthless to anyone but Camille."

Owen and I exchanged a look.

"And just one more thing," Owen said. "When was the last time you saw Camille?"

Lou looked at me as he answered. "Again, it was the last time I saw you. When she fired me."

I nodded, but Owen had more questions. "And getting fired right before the show must've been pretty unexpected, right?"

"No one expects to be fired," Lou said, sounding a little sad. "But the timing was surprising, yeah."

"Were you angry with Camille?" Owen asked.

Lou narrowed his eyes at Owen. "Yes, a little bit. But that was nothing new. The woman operated on making people angry. If she wasn't blackmailing you or firing you, she was digging into your past and threatening to expose all your secrets."

"Oh," Owen said, clearly surprised. "Did she do any of that to you?"

The man across the table shook his head. "I don't have many secrets," he said. "Not like some folks on the circuit. I've never pretended to be anything I'm not."

"And other people who knew Camille have been pretending?" I asked.

He lifted a shoulder. "Not for me to say. Is this about more than just Beau going missing?"

Owen studied Lou for a moment, and then said, "Mr. Grant, Camille Hawthorne was found dead at the Paw Spa the morning after she let you go."

Grant straightened and his mouth dropped open. "Wait, are you accusing me of killing her?"

"Not at all," Owen replied. "But we are investigating her death and wanted to gather whatever information you might be able to share. Is there anything else you think we need to know?"

"Well, I didn't do it," he said. "And weirdly, I feel kind of sad to learn about it. She wasn't nice... but she didn't deserve to die either."

"Do you remember where you were the rest of that evening?" Owen asked him.

"I went to the bar down in Hammer Cove. I was there all night, and then I was home with my girlfriend, Alice."

"And will someone at the bar be able to corroborate your presence there?" Owen asked.

"The owner, Curt. I sat at the bar, and we chatted for hours. And then Alice, of course." Lou took the paper Owen offered and scrolled through his phone to find the numbers to write down.

"Mr. Grant, I think that will be all for today," Owen said, pushing his chair back and standing. He reached a hand out to shake one of Mr. Grant's and then thanked him for his time. "If we have further questions, would you mind if we called?"

"Given that you're the police, I don't feel like I have the option to say no, do I?"

Owen smiled at him and shook his head.

"And I trust you're going to figure out who the heck is framing me as a dognapper?"

"We'll do our best," Owen said as he walked the man out.

When Mr. Grant was gone, Owen turned to me. "What do you think?"

"I'm inclined to believe him," I told Owen. "And I'm guessing Marla is the one who chose his name as 'Sam's' owner."

Owen nodded. "Me too. I'll just verify his alibi." He pressed his lips together and looked farther down the hall. "Marla is in Interrogation room two."

We entered the room and took seats across from the woman I had met at the Regal Retreat the night before.

"Ms. Carver," Owen said, his easy smile back in place. "Can you tell us one more time, for the record, about the

Borzoi that was checked into the Regal Retreat two days ago?"

Marla let out an exasperated sigh, rolling her eyes. "I told you already—the dog, Sam, was checked in by a man named Lou Grant."

"We've spoken to Mr. Grant, and he has no recollection of checking in this dog. He also does not own a dog named Sam," Owen said.

"Well," Marla said, her voice taking on a tone that suggested she was being as reasonable as possible, "someone is lying."

"Do you make a habit of taking in dogs without verifying their ownership?" Owen asked.

Marla scowled at him. "As you can imagine, with the dog show in town, the Regal Retreat is extremely busy right now. I may not have had time to be as diligent as I usually am. But regardless of what you may have heard, the Regal Retreat is a very well-respected establishment. We take only the very best dogs, and I was certain anyone owning a Borzoi would have credible ownership papers."

"What do you mean, regardless of what we may have heard?" I asked her.

Marla's eyes slid to me. "Only that there have been some rumors in the last year or two about my business. All untrue, of course."

Owen leaned back, raising an eyebrow. "What kind of rumors?"

"The kind evil women spread when they don't like you. The kind that just aren't true."

Owen and I exchanged a look.

"What women don't like you?" I asked.

Marla frowned. "A few years ago, I had a dog that took Best in Show at the Humboldt Dog Show. It was a stunning victory that no one expected—especially those with dogs who are usually favored to win."

"What kind of dog was it?" Owen asked with interest.

"It was an Irish wolfhound. His name was Franz. Unfortunately, he died last year."

My heart ached with sympathy. "I'm so sorry."

Marla nodded, sadness etched into every line around her eyes.

"So people like Camille Hawthorne, for instance, might have been upset about this victory?" Owen asked.

Marla let out a frustrated breath. "Among others. But yes, Camille was particularly vindictive about the whole thing. It seems she didn't think we won fairly, and so she set out to try to ruin my business. She was also angry about a previous disagreement."

"What was that?" I asked.

"She'd booked a reservation but then cancelled at the last minute. I kept her deposit. Standard practice."

"Seems fair," I said. We did the same thing at the inn.

"She didn't see it that way. She did her best to ruin me."

"By doing what?" Owen asked.

"You name it," Marla said, waving a hand in the air. "Mostly just did what she does best, spread rumors that aren't true. She told people the dogs who stayed at the Regal Retreat were neglected, kept in unsanitary conditions, didn't get fed on schedule. She talked and talked—enough that my business declined, and I almost had to shut down."

Owen nodded with sympathy, then asked, "Marla, did you have anything to do with Beaumont Royale's disappearance?"

Marla glanced between us but stuck to her story. "Of course not. As I told you, the dog checked into the Regal Retreat may be Beaumont Royale, but I was told his name was Sam. I don't make a habit of questioning my customers. They pay way too much for that."

"The dog is most likely Beaumont Royale," Owen said. "We just need to check his microchip to confirm it."

Marla didn't say anything after that. She looked between us with something like alarm in her eyes.

"Marla, did you have a romantic entanglement with Camille Hawthorne's handler a few years ago?" Owen asked.

The woman's eyes narrowed and her lips pursed. She said nothing for a long moment, and I thought she would deny it, but then she nodded once. "I did."

"What was his name?" Owen pressed.

Marla's eyes dropped to the table. "Lou Grant."

"Was that the same Lou who checked in the Borzoi Sam?" Owen asked this question innocently, as if he hadn't just caught Marla in his trap.

She sniffed, but didn't answer. "Are you charging me with something?" she asked finally.

Owen shook his head, letting out an affable chuckle, and I was amazed yet again at how he maintained his easygoing attitude, even in the face of criminal activity. "No, Marla, you're free to go. Please don't leave town, though."

I wondered what would happen to Beaumont Royale now that Camille was gone. But I didn't have time to ask Owen, as we ushered Marla out and the officer from the front informed us that Nina Reyes would be waiting in Interrogation room one.

This was turning into a full-day affair.

Owen and I headed into interrogation room one once again. This time, Nina Reyes sat across the table, her hands clasped in front of her. She wore a silver ring on her right index finger, which she was turning around and around. As we entered, she looked up at us, her eyes darting between Owen and me.

"Nina, thank you so much for joining us. I know we've asked you a few questions already, but we hope you won't mind a few more. Dahlia is working in an official capacity at this point on this investigation," Owen said.

"I'm happy to help, but I swear I've told you everything I know." Nina's hands continued clutching one another on the table.

"I have a new question for you, based on the invoices you handed us yesterday."

Nina focused her attention on Owen, her hands stilling.

"The invoice for Camille Hawthorne was unpaid," he said slowly. "Even though it was from several months back. Did Camille often leave her bills unpaid?"

Nina's eyes flicked between Owen's face and mine before landing back on his and relaxing somewhat. "Oh, that. Yes, I didn't hold Camille to her payments. I was doing her a favor. She was struggling a little bit." She leaned in and whispered the next word. "Financially." Nina's words seemed to confirm my suspicion that Camille might not have been as well off as she had positioned herself to be. But something about Nina's demeanor made me uncertain.

"How long had you been allowing Camille to enjoy spa services without paying for them?" I asked her.

Nina's head tilted slightly, and she glanced upward as

if looking back in her memory. "A year or two, I suppose. I'd have to look at my records."

"Please do let us know," Owen said. "Are there any other clients for whom you've waived fees?"

"Now and then, I suppose. But nothing regular."

"Nothing as regular as the way you waived them for Camille."

Nina swallowed audibly. "Right."

Owen nodded but said nothing else.

"Do you know who did it yet? Who killed Camille?" Nina asked, looking between Owen and me again.

"We'll be in touch," Owen said, as if the question hadn't been asked at all. He rose from the table and gestured Nina to the door. He walked Nina back to the front, and then we met in the hallway.

"My office?" he asked, nodding toward his doorway at the end of the hall.

I headed inside and took a seat in the leather armchair across from his desk.

"Okay," he said. "So, what do we know?"

I thought for a moment. I didn't feel like we had really learned anything new, but maybe we had verified a couple of things. "Well, we have almost definitive proof that the dog at the retreat is Beaumont Royale."

"Actually, we *do* have proof."

"I thought we were waiting for the chip to get read?"

"I had an officer take him to a vet this morning to read

the chip. That's Beaumont Royale. I just wanted to see if Marla would admit it."

"Okay... so we found Beau, that's good. But if Lou Grant is telling the truth, then he's being framed." I tapped my finger to my lips. "You think Marla knew that dog wasn't Sam?"

Owen shrugged. "I'm thinking she most likely did. She also gave us a decent motive for hurting Camille."

"The rumors," I remembered.

"Right," Owen said. "But Lou had a motive too—he was just let go."

"He insists he is being framed," I said, thinking aloud.

"And I'm inclined to believe him. We just need to check his alibi. Owen made a note on the notepad in front of him. "I've spoken to the other people who had a door code to the Paw Spa, and verified their alibis. The only person I haven't been able to get ahold of is Victoria Dane, but I'm working on that. What else?" he asked.

"Well, there's Camille's finances. Didn't Nina seem uncomfortable talking about that?"

Owen nodded. "She did. And I find it hard to believe that Camille Hawthorne was struggling, but we requested access to her banking records and should have those soon if we don't already. That ought to answer that question."

"We still really don't know what happened to Camille. Only that someone took her dog, she sustained a head injury, and she drowned." I wanted to understand what had happened. I didn't particularly like Camille, but I hated the idea of an injustice having been done to her with no repercussions at all.

"The question is whether those three things all happened at once, or if they were separate incidents," Owen said.

"The footage from the security camera should help, right?" I pointed out.

"As long as everyone came and went through the front door. I've got a few calls into IT about that and Camille's cell phone. We should have everything we can get from both of those soon."

That was smart. I hadn't thought about her phone. "The phone will tell us where she's been the last couple days, I guess. And with whom." I didn't use mine as much as most people seemed to, and even so, my phone definitely acted as both a diary and a kind of tracking device.

"Definitely. Let me check on that stuff now." Owen raised a finger, then picked up the phone on his desk and punched in a few numbers. "Tristan, how are we doing with that phone and security footage from the Paw Spa?"

Owen listened for a few moments, nodding his head. "Let me know when you have it." He hung up the phone and looked at me. "IT says we should have full records from the phone and the timestamped footage by tomorrow morning."

"So... nothing to do between now and then, I guess," I said.

Owen raised an eyebrow and smiled at me. "I think you're forgetting—you have an inn to run."

I did. And I knew I needed to be getting back to it.

"I'll check on Lou's alibis and see if we can get access to Camille's summer house. Maybe we'll find something there..."

"Okay," I said, rising to go. "I'll talk to you soon."

Chapter Ten

When I returned to the inn that evening, I felt a twinge of guilt for having been gone so much recently. The lobby was populated with guests and dogs, many of them chatting excitedly about the upcoming weekend's events. Amal was busy at the reception desk, flicking through reservation screens for the coming days. She glanced up when I came through the front door, and Taco leaped from his curled-up position near the desk to greet me. I felt like I'd been neglecting them both.

"Is everything going all right?" I asked Amal.

"I was going to ask you the same thing." I knelt and gave Taco some attention before moving to chat with Amal closer to the desk. "Everything is going as well as can be expected, I suppose—when you're investigating a murder, that is. But I feel like I've been neglecting my responsibilities here. Are we full?"

"We will be tomorrow. The last guests are checking in tomorrow morning."

I didn't want to abandon Amal, but I did need to prepare breakfast for the morning. Though I was always up early, there was a lot I could do ahead of time. Normally, I had things waiting in the refrigerator inside the apartment to pop into the oven, but my involvement with Camille's murder had me running behind despite my best efforts.

I lingered in the lobby, tidying up and chatting with guests about Saltcliff's local attractions and about their dogs. As the evening wore on, the lobby began to empty as guests retired to their suites. Finally, Taco, Amal, and I were the only ones left in the cozy, fire-lit space.

"You can head home," I told Amal, worried she'd spent more time here today than she should have already.

"Actually, I was wondering if you might want to talk for a while?"

I knew Amal had been worried about something and wondered if she was finally going to tell me what it was. "I'd like that. Only, I do need to do a bit of baking. Would you be willing to chat in the kitchen?" I asked hopefully. "I'll even pour you a glass of wine while we do it."

"That sounds lovely."

Amal and I finished tidying the lobby, then she

followed me through the apartment door, Taco on her heels.

"Taco!" Diantha popped her head out of her room, gave us a smile, and then ushered Taco inside, shutting her door again.

As I pulled together my favorite chai scones, Amal sipped from her glass at the little round table in the corner. Silence between us was not unusual, and I knew she would fill it when she was ready.

"So the investigation is going well?"

"I guess so," I told her. "It feels strange to be such an official part of it. Strange, but good."

Just then, a burst of laughter came from Diantha's room. Amal raised an eyebrow and grinned at me. "More training?"

"I expect so," I told her. "Danny says she's got several new tricks to show us soon."

"Maybe she's taught Taco how to tell jokes," Amal said.

I frowned at her. Taco could not speak. "I doubt that very much."

As I cut open a long vanilla bean and used the edge of the knife to push the seeds into the bowl, Amal cleared her throat. "Dahlia, I wondered..." Amal paused, and I waited. "If I were to take an extended trip, do you think you'd be able to do without me for a bit?"

I glanced at her over my shoulder. "Extended trip? Where are you going?"

"Probably nowhere," she said. "But my cousin is getting married, and I've been invited to go home to attend."

"You just told me how much you love weddings," I reminded her. "Why wouldn't you attend?"

"Well, for one thing, it's in India. For another, I'm just not sure I want to go back."

I mixed the dough with my hands and shaped it into scones on a tray. As I pulled plastic over them, I thought about what Amal had said—and what she hadn't said. I washed my hands and joined her at the table, pouring a tiny bit of wine into a second glass for myself. "Are you and your cousin very close?"

Amal smiled. "My cousin was a baby when I left," she said. "Remember, I'm an old spinster. A woman of a certain age, worried about bone density and protein."

"Those things are important," I reminded her.

Amal laughed. "I was making a joke, Dahlia. But there's no denying that at my age, and in my family, it's very unusual for a woman to live the way I do."

"You make it sound like you're a bank robber or some-thing. I'm sure your family is very proud of you."

Amal smiled, but it wasn't a happy expression. She took a long sip of her wine, then peered into the glass as she set it back on the table, her forehead creasing. "Proud is not the word that I would use," she said. "In fact, I was very surprised to receive the invitation."

"I'm probably not the best person to offer advice here," I told her. "My sister and I hadn't talked in ten years when she died. I don't know a lot about mending family rifts or meeting expectations from relatives."

Amal sighed and leaned back in her chair. "I know that," she said. "But Dahlia, I value your opinion. You're wise and steady, and you're my best friend. I just wanted to share what I've been thinking about."

My friend's words touched my heart, and I felt awkward for a moment as I searched for words that would be appropriate. "When do you need to decide?"

"Not for a while," Amal said. "But I think it's going to take me a little bit of time to decide how I feel about the prospect of facing everyone again. One of my aunts especially disapproved of my decision to leave home."

"Well, to answer your original question, we will be fine without you. We will miss you, but as long as no one gets murdered while you're gone, I should be able to hold down the fort."

Amal laughed and raised an eyebrow at me. We talked about other things for another half hour before my friend finally decided it was time she headed home. She hugged me, and I told her I'd see her in the morning.

The next morning, I put out breakfast for the guests, then took Taco with me on a walk to the police station. More and more, I was having to tackle several tasks at once to keep up with everything expected of me. Poor Taco would have to sit through a quick meeting with Owen, who had texted me early to tell me that he had Camille's financial records and wanted to show me something.

In Owen's office, financial statements were spread across the entire surface of his desk, and as I settled into the chair across from his, my eyes roamed over the numbers. The balances quoted on Camille Hawthorne's investment and bank accounts were not those of a woman struggling financially.

"So if Nina wasn't letting her skip payments because she was doing a good deed, why was she letting her get away without paying?" I asked Owen.

He was still standing, leaning over the statements, and now he straightened, spreading his arms wide and shaking his head. "I have no idea. Unless Camille demanded that Nina provide services without charging her."

"I don't think that's how businesses work, Owen. Otherwise, I could just go to a restaurant and demand that they give me lunch without paying."

"Only if you had something you could use for leverage."

Leverage. I hadn't thought of that. "So you think Camille had something on Nina?"

Owen nodded. "It's one explanation. It would also explain this." He pointed to a checking statement with a deposit listed from the Paw Spa. "And this, and this." His finger moved down the page, stopping briefly at several deposits over the past few months, each for five hundred dollars, each from the Paw Spa.

"Nina was paying Camille!" The question was, what did Camille have on Nina?

"I think we need to start looking at Nina Reyes as a real suspect." Owen looked grim as he said this, as if he were sad to have to think of anyone as an actual suspect in a murder case.

"So we just need to figure out what it was Camille might've been holding over her head."

Owen nodded. "And as with all things in investigations, that's easier said than done. And she's not our only lead based on what's in here," he said, returning his gaze to the reports.

"What else is in there?"

"Regular payments to Lou Grant."

"He was her employee, actually," I pointed out.

"True, so those may be legitimate. What about to Elliott Nazar?"

I thought for a moment. "Wait, the guest at the inn? The one who left suddenly."

"He's a dog show judge," Owen said.

"She was paying him?"

Owen nodded, flipping through pages. "For years, actually."

That was definitely strange. "Sounds like we need to talk with Mr. Nazar."

"Working on it."

Taco and I walked quickly back though town, taking a quick detour to say hello to Valerie at Beachside Bakes. I didn't really have time to pop in, but I hadn't seen Valerie in at least a week, and I felt I should say hello. More and more, my sense that I was juggling too many responsibilities threatened to overwhelm me. I was enjoying my time as an official consultant to the Saltcliff Police Department, but I still wasn't sure I could do all the things I needed to do and do them all well. It was an interesting problem.

"Hi Doll! Hello, Taco Doggy!" Valerie had just rung up a customer and as he proceeded outside to a table in the sun, she came around the counter to give me a hug and to offer Taco a dog cookie.

"Hi Valerie," I said, glad to see my friend looking well. Her curly red hair was half up, pulled back from her fair face and emphasizing her blue eyes. She wore bright colors, as she usually did. Today's ensemble was a deep royal blue with a coral necklace and jeans. "How are you doing?"

Valerie laughed and raised her arms as if to indicate the bakery. "Same as usual. Life is good, you know?"

"It is," I agreed.

"Do you have time for tea, or did you just pop in to say hi?"

"I'd love a cup of tea," I said, feeling like I shouldn't linger, but tempted by the homey feeling inside Beachside Bakes and the company of my friend. "But we should be quick."

"Lots going on?" Valerie asked, moving back behind the counter to make the tea. I settled at a table just inside the window, Taco at my feet.

"Definitely. More than I'm used to." As Valerie settled across from me, a piece of her lemon cake between us with two forks, I told her about my engagement with the police department and about the case. Then I told her about Diantha's involvement in the dog show and the fact we were full at the inn. There had never been a previous time in my life when I had been so needed in so many places. "I guess I'm just feeling a little bit stressed."

"Dahlia," Valerie said thoughtfully, "I think you're just

feeling what it is to have a full load of friends and family who you care about."

Maybe she was right. I didn't have a lot of people in my life before moving here. And while people brought responsibilities, I found that I didn't mind them one bit. It was just... different.

"I think you're right. I just don't want to let anyone down."

Valerie smiled at me. "I don't think you're capable. You're one of the most conscientious people I've ever met. You take responsibility seriously, and that includes responsibilities to people."

"Thanks, Valerie."

We talked a bit more, and then Taco and I thanked my friend and we headed back toward the inn.

As Taco and I passed through my adopted hometown, nodding at familiar faces and breathing in the fresh, salty sea air, I acknowledged that it was a good concern to have. Maybe I was just growing used to this new life I had found. Maybe I couldn't do it all, but I could do the things I wanted to. And I wanted to help Owen. And I wanted to be there for Diantha and Amal.

Taco and I entered the lobby, expecting to find it calm and peaceful as it usually was just before the lunchtime hour. I had fallen into the rhythm of running a bed-and-breakfast, and it seemed that after breakfast, people tended to linger for a bit before heading to their rooms to prepare for whatever activities they had planned for the day. But when I stepped into the lobby of the Saltcliff Inn that morning, peace was not what I found.

Instead, I discovered my niece sitting on the couch, chattering excitedly with Emerson and two other guests whom I had been introduced to but whose names I didn't recall. They turned to acknowledge me as Taco and I came in, and Diantha jumped to her feet.

"Here he is!" She rushed toward Taco and lavished him with kisses all over his big square head. Taco did not seem surprised by this behavior, nor was he put off by the sudden show of affection. Instead, he trotted back with her to the group seated on the couch, who all eagerly patted him and spoke to him in happy voices.

I stepped closer, hoping to understand what had brought on this show of affection for my service dog.

"So this is the famous Taco Dog," Emerson said, grinning up at me.

"Uh... yes."

"I've been telling them about all the tricks he's been learning," Diantha said, "and they've been giving me tips on how best to show him at the competition this weekend."

"Well, that's great."

Diantha, I knew, made friends very easily. Sometimes I envied her lack of self-consciousness and innate confidence. I didn't regret my life now, but if I had grown up with her total ease in the world of people, my life might have looked very different.

"Aunt Dolly," she said, standing and clasping her hands in front of her chest, "I was hoping that maybe I could do a little show this evening, sort of a warm-up for the dog show?"

Another woman sitting on the couch clapped her hands eagerly and shrilled, "Oh yes, that would be wonderful!"

"Then I can get some hands-on critique from the experts," Diantha said, nodding at the women on the couch.

"Well, I suppose if Taco is up for that, then I don't have a problem with it."

"Would you mind if I move some of the furniture around in the lobby?"

I glanced around the lobby, which, in my estimation, was perfectly arranged. Of course, it was arranged to be the lobby of a bed and breakfast, not to be the showplace for a young girl and a dog showing off their tricks. "I think that would be okay."

I tried to hide the hesitation that came naturally to me, but Diantha didn't seem to hear it either way. She clapped her hands and looked down fondly at my dog.

"Okay, Taco," she said. "Dress rehearsal tonight. Be ready."

I had the sense Taco was pretty much always ready for whatever Diantha wanted him to do. Now, she patted his head, then turned back to the ladies on the couch as she led him to the apartment door. "We're gonna have to go practice now," she said. Then she seemed to think of something and looked at me. "Is that okay, Aunt Dolly? Do you need him today?"

I shook my head. The only time I strictly required Taco's assistance was at restaurants, and one thing I definitely did not have time for at the moment was eating out at new establishments that might use legumes in their meals.

"Okay, we'll be inside." My niece and my dog disappeared through the adjoining door.

"She's a wonderful girl," the woman who had enthusiastically celebrated Diantha's idea for a showcase said. "I've raised four daughters myself, and I can tell you—girls aren't always the easiest. But you've obviously done a great job with Danny."

"Thank you," I told her. While a tiny glow of pride threatened to light inside me, it was immediately doused by the guilt I felt at taking any credit for my sister's obvious good parenting. "She's my sister's daughter," I explained. "I'm just her guardian."

The woman stood and placed her hands on her very round hips. She looked angry as she said, "Don't you do that. You're not 'just' anything. You are the person she depends on and the person who is raising her now. You take credit, because parenting is not easy."

I felt chastened, but also... better. "Thank you, Ms....?"

"I'm Anita Boyle. I'm showing my dog, Remington, this weekend."

"The Pekingese," Emerson said helpfully. Emerson's dog, the nervous Sir Edgar, had been sitting on her lap this whole time, notably more relaxed than he was the evening he arrived. The other ladies' dogs must have been napping in their rooms, because they were not with them.

The women gazed at me expectantly, and I realized I had an opportunity here to learn a bit more about dog show culture, and maybe about our suspects.

"Ladies, might I ask you a question or two?" I tried, taking a nervous step nearer. "About dog shows?"

"Certainly," the red-haired woman said, sitting back down. "Join us."

I barely managed a question before I was being schooled on every aspect of showing champion dogs. I listened carefully for the better part of an hour before several of the women rose, excusing themselves. I was left sitting with Emerson, who grinned at me. "More than you ever wanted to know, I bet," she said.

"It was a lot," I agreed, "but very informative. There was one more thing though..."

"I'll help if I can," she said, putting Sir Edgar on the

floor where he began tentatively sniffing around the legs of the coffee table.

"I wondered if you were familiar with the judge who was here, Elliott Nazar?"

"I know about all the judges," Emerson said. "I've been studying for the day when Sir Edgar is ready."

"Can you share what you've learned about Mr. Nazar?" I asked.

She nodded. "He grew up in South Chicago," she said. "In a very poor family."

"That doesn't sound like typical dog show material," I said.

"Oh no, it wasn't. He was a real rags to riches kind of story, I gather. And when he joined the circuit, it was as if he'd always been there. He knew all the dogs, the owners, all the dirt..."

"The dirt?" I pressed.

"Oh, you know. Dog owners are always spreading gossip about one another."

"Like Camille Hawthorne and Victoria Dane?" I asked.

Emerson smiled and nodded. "And Camille knew everything about everyone," she said. "She and Elliott were... close."

"Was that typical? For contestants to be close to judges?"

"Not really," Emerson said. "But it seemed like Beaumont Royale was just drawn to Elliott. There was an article about it somewhere that I read. That was how he got into judging, I guess. I can't remember all the details."

I made a mental note to track down that article. "That is interesting, thank you."

"Any time," she said, rising. "I better get Sir Edgar out for a walk before he lets loose in your lobby again. Nice chatting with you."

I returned to the desk and did a quick search online, quickly locating the article Emerson had mentioned in Dogs Today, a show magazine published quarterly. The piece profiled several judges including Mr. Nazar, revealing that he'd entered the dog show world through Camille Hawthorne.

"He was a dog walker when he met Beaumont Royale," she was quoted as saying. "Very rough and tumble. But he knew everything there was to know about dogs, and Beau loved him."

According to the article, she suggested he pursue a career in judging, and he never looked back.

I flipped through a few more search results, finding a list of shows where Elliott had been a judge.

"Well, that's definitely interesting," I whispered as I noticed something. I was about to dig a bit deeper when my phone rang. I pulled it from my pocket to answer the call from Owen. "Hello?"

"Hi, Dahlia. Do you want the short version or the long version?" Owen sounded merry as he asked this question.

"I guess I better take the short version. I feel like there's a lot going on here at the inn. Plus, I've got news for you too."

"Oh great. Why don't you give me yours first?"

"I've just learned that Elliott Nazar became a dog show judge because Camille Hawthorne led him to it," I told Owen.

"Interesting," he said. "There could be something there, I guess."

"I think there is because there's one more thing. I found a list of all the shows he's judged and a list of the winners in each category at each of those shows. Beaumont Royale almost always wins if Nazar is judging."

"Oh, good work," Owen said. "We'll need to dig a little deeper into that. I've got calls out looking for Nazar. He's a tough guy to track down. Any other news on your end?"

"No, that was it."

"Okay, well, I've got everything back from the IT department. We've got a sequence of comings and goings from the Paw Spa on the night of Camille Hawthorne's murder. And I've also got some interesting information gathered from her phone. Which would you like first?"

That *was* exciting.

"Tell me what was on her phone," I said, smiling at Amal, who had just appeared from the back of the hotel.

"Okay, well, I *think* I know why she was at the Paw Spa."

"Why was she there?"

"Victoria Dane asked her to meet. After hours. Evidently, they both had the code to the front door, and Victoria said in her text that it was 'neutral territory,' whatever that means."

Victoria Dane. Owen had interviewed her briefly, since she was one of the people who had been in the spa the day of Camille's death. But she had no information to offer and had been bumped down on the list of suspects, along with Derek and Juliette, who both worked at the Paw Spa.

"Yes, but that wasn't the only interesting text she received the night of her death."

"What else?"

"There's another text. From someone labeled in her phone as Regal Rascal."

"Regal Rascal? A nickname for someone?"

"I assume so. It should be easy enough to find out who by matching the number. And we need to do that, because what came from Regal Rascal was a ransom note."

"For Beaumont Royale!" I said excitedly. Now we were finally getting somewhere.

"Yes, exactly. But the ransom came in the morning. Hours after the coroner says Camille was already dead."

I thought about that for a minute. "So whoever dognapped Beau didn't know Camille was dead."

"Most likely not," Owen said. "Unless it was the killer trying to seem like they weren't the killer."

"That seems unlikely." Of course I had no real idea how killers thought. But it still didn't make sense to me.

"I agree." Owen paused, then continued. "And we also have the footage from the security camera on the front door that shows who came and went that night."

"Oh, excellent. Learn anything from that?"

"The first person we see is Marla Carver, right around eight-thirty. And then Camille and Victoria arrived soon after she did."

That was interesting. "So all three of them were there at once?"

"Maybe," Owen said, sounding thoughtful. "But the footage shows Victoria leaving not much later. And neither Camille nor Marla are shown leaving at all."

Well. It made sense that Camille hadn't left. "So we have no idea how long Marla was there," I said.

"And it seems to solidify the idea that she is the dognapper. She took him out the back door."

"Right," I said, wondering what exactly had gone on in that spa the night Camille died.

"The footage also catches someone—a man—arriving but not entering. He pauses, as if looking through the glass on the door, but then leaves without going in."

"Just a passerby, I guess?"

"Maybe."

"Can we identify him?"

"We're working on that. We also have a few comings and goings in the morning hours," Owen said. "We see Derek arriving quite early in the morning and then immediately stepping back outside and having a chat on his phone in the camera's line of sight. Then he waits a bit and Nina appears, and they go in together."

"That's when they discover the body," I say.

"Right. And Derek discovered the front door unlocked and called Nina."

"So Derek was the first one inside after all the nighttime activities," I said.

"Unless someone came in through the back door," Owen said.

I blew out a breath. Where did that leave us? "So we need to talk to Victoria, Derek, and Nina again, then?"

"Looks like. I'm particularly interested in Victoria at this point. She hasn't returned any calls, and I haven't had luck finding her at home." Owen said. "I'll let you know what I find out."

"Thanks. Good night, Owen."

Despite Victoria's elusiveness, I hung up the phone feeling like we had finally made some real progress.

Chapter Eleven

That evening, Diantha set up the lobby with a clear area in the front near the fire and the furniture angled around it in a half circle. She'd created and printed invitations to slide under every guest room door, inviting them to a fun rehearsal performance of Taco Dog's tricks.

I wasn't honestly sure how many of these fancy dog aficionados would show up, based on the education I'd received this week about how very seriously "real" dog people took these shows, but I was relieved to see almost every guest in attendance, and plenty of canine companions.

I'd made mini bundt cakes and toffee for the event, and there was a wine and soda bar set up at one side of the room.

As people milled around before the show began, Diantha stood at my side in the back, Taco at our feet.

"I'm nervous, Aunt Dolly," she said, rubbing her hands together. "My stomach feels like it's turning inside out."

"I know that feeling," I told her. "It's no fun, but it's pretty normal. Just try to take some deep breaths and remember why you decided to do this."

"That's good advice, Dahlia," Amal said. "As a child, I got very nervous any time I was in front of a group, and my father always said the same thing. He said if you close your eyes for a moment and focus on the outcome, you'll be in tune with your purpose. And when you're in tune with your purpose, everything else falls away."

Diantha looked between us with a skeptical frown, but she let her eyes fall shut and I watched her chest fill with deep breaths. After a few moments, she opened her eyes again.

"Better?" I asked.

She shrugged. "Maybe?"

I looked around the room. Most of the guests had found seats and were snacking on the treats we'd put out. "I think it's time, Danny."

She nodded and took one more deep breath. "Okay."

My niece marched to the front of the room after telling Taco to stay put. Once there, she looked around with a smile. When the crowd had quieted, she took one more deep breath, and then in a confident voice, she began speaking.

"Hello everyone. I'm Danny Vale, and I'm so happy to see so many accomplished dog owners, showers, and handlers here tonight. I will be showing my aunt's service dog Taco at the dog show this weekend in two of the amateur categories. I hoped that we could show you what we've been working on and maybe take a few suggestions for how we might improve our work."

She looked around with eager eyes, and a few people exclaimed from the gathered group, "Of course!" And "We'd love to help!"

"Great," she said. "I guess we'll get started then." She smiled up at me over the heads seated before her, and then she said in a clear loud voice, "Taco. Come."

My dog sprang to his feet and trotted happily to the front of the room where Diantha waited for him.

"Taco. Sit."

He did as he was told, dropping into a sit at her side and smiling out at the crowd. She slipped him a treat from her pocket, which he devoured greedily before resuming his nonchalant pose.

"Taco Dog has been trained as a service dog, to help my aunt avoid specific allergens that are dangerous for her," she told the crowd. "He is a purebred English Chocolate Labrador Retriever, and as you can surely see, he is a good boy."

There was a light ripple of laughter through the crowd at this.

"I have been working with him for only a short time, and he has managed to learn more tricks than even I thought he'd be able to. The first one that we'll demonstrate for you is related to his service job. We call it 'Find.'" Taco perked up at the word find, and stared up at Diantha. "Earlier today, Emerson gave me an item that belongs to Sir Edgar, her Frenchie puppy. We hid it somewhere in this room. Now," she said, holding up a piece of fabric that she pulled from her pocket, "I'll let Taco sniff this cloth with Sir Edgar's scent on it, and he'll find the toy."

Diantha bent down and held out the cloth. "Taco. Find."

Taco eagerly sniffed at the cloth, and after a moment's confusion, in which he tried to eat it, he seemed to understand the command. He dropped his nose to the ground as I'd seen him do before, and began searching the lobby. After a few minutes and a very thorough inspection of many of the audience members and their canine companions, he stopped next to a bookshelf on the far side of the room and barked his alert.

"One bark means he has found something," Diantha explained, skipping over to where Taco waited. She encouraged him, and he nosed at the first shelf of books, where she found the toy after moving a few books aside. The crowd burst into applause.

"Taco actually performed that same trick in service to the local police," Diantha said as she moved back to the front of the room. "He helped them solve part of a mystery."

The crowd clapped again, and Taco looked more pleased with himself than I'd ever seen him.

The duo ran through a few more tricks, which the crowd seemed to enjoy, and Diantha then had him sit at her side. "Up!" she said, pointing at the coffee table.

As Taco leapt atop the table, I realized I should have paid more attention to the tricks and the items required for them. Surely, we could have found a box or a stool for Taco to jump on. I made a mental note to give the table top an extra cleaning tonight before bed.

It was from his proudly elevated position that Taco beamed out at the crowd as Diantha gave him his final treat.

"That concludes our show," she said, smiling widely. "I'd be more than happy to hear your thoughts and suggestions, but wanted to let you know that it's also totally fine to just go. Thank you all so much for your time."

There was a long enthusiastic round of applause, and a few barks here and there from the four-legged audience members. Soon, most people were up out of their seats, getting more to eat or excusing themselves for the night. I was happy to see a few people chatting with Diantha. The show had been a success.

Taco was so riled up after his exhibition, I decided to take him out for an evening walk, even though I was tired myself. Diantha was also practically bouncing off the walls, but she had several people eager to chat with her after the show ended, so I quietly snapped Taco's leash on and let him out the front door, letting Amal know that I would be back quickly so she could depart.

Taco and I walked along the quiet, dark streets of Saltcilff and I praised him gently for the way he had handled his part of the show tonight. Part of my growing admiration for my dog had to do with the fact that he seemed to know that his performance contributed directly to my niece's sense of confidence. And he seemed just as invested in taking care of Diantha as I was.

As we turned up Main Street, I waved and smiled to the few people out also enjoying the evening air.

One person was walking toward me along the sidewalk, a hood pulled over her head obscuring her face. I knew it was a woman by the way she walked, and there was something familiar about her. As we drew closer, the woman turned her head away from me, but I caught a flash of the long red hair pouring out of the hood. I'd only ever met one person with hair that color besides Valerie, who ran Beachside Bakes. And this was not Valerie.

"Victoria?" I asked. The figure stopped and the face turned toward me. Victoria Dane's hands lifted to push the hood off her head, and though she appeared somewhat flustered, she greeted me with a smile. "Oh hello there," she said.

"We met at the Paw Spa, I'm Dahlia Vale, and this is Taco."

"Oh yes, I remember you." Victoria reached a hand out to Taco, who sniffed her eagerly before dropping into a sit and gazing up at us both.

Victoria seemed about to resume her walk, but I knew I needed to ask her a few questions, since Owen mentioned he'd had trouble tracking her down.

"I wondered, could I...?" I wasn't sure exactly what to ask her.

Victoria paused and turned back to me, anxiety lining her face. She shook her head slightly as if in question, and I hurried to form a coherent thought.

"I just wondered, did you go back to the Paw Spa that day that I saw you there? Maybe in the evening after hours?"

"What? Why would I do that?"

I hadn't expected her to deny it. I shifted my weight but kept my gaze locked on hers. "It's only that they have a security camera on the front door. I don't know if you knew that."

Victoria's mouth dropped open slightly and she cleared her throat and pushed her hair away from her face with one hand. "Oh. That's right, I did go back, I forgot something." Then Victoria frowned at me, her eyebrows drawing angry lines above her eyes. "What is this about anyway?"

"Well, I run the Saltcliff B&B, but I also consult for the police department."

Now Victoria's eyebrows climbed practically to her red hairline. "The police department?"

"Yes, and I'm helping look into the circumstances surrounding Camille Hawthorn's death. You don't know anything about that, do you?"

Victoria pressed a hand to her chest and made a little gasping sound. "This seems very inappropriate, Dahlia," she said, lifting her chin into the air and gazing around her. "I am a citizen out on an evening walk, and I don't think it's right for me to be questioned on the sidewalk."

"I agree actually, shall we meet at the police station tomorrow morning?"

Victoria's lips pressed into a hard line, and she said nothing for a moment. I sensed that she knew she'd been cornered. And beyond that, I began to think that I might be chatting with a murderer.

"I'm very busy tomorrow."

"Why don't you suggest a time that would work then?" I said.

Victoria huffed out a little breath and then relented. "Fine. Nine o'clock will work. I'll be there." She didn't say goodbye as she strolled away from me, not bothering to lift her hood again.

Taco and I exchanged a glance. "I think I just did some police work, Taco." I pulled out my phone and texted Owen quickly to let him know of the development.

Owen: great job, Dahlia!

As I went to bed that night, I felt a spark of pride. I loved the feeling of actually accomplishing goals and getting things done. And I felt like I had really helped in this case so far.

Chapter Twelve

At nine o'clock the following morning, I used my new badge to enter the police department lobby and then waited for the officer at the desk to open the door to the back so that Taco and I could enter the interrogation room where Victoria Dane was waiting.

Owen met us in the hallway.

"Great work tracking down Victoria," Owen said again, setting that pride glowing within me once more. "I've finally got some information about Elliott Nazar, too."

"Is he coming in?"

"I haven't found him yet, but there's some interesting information to share. Can you stay for a bit when we're done here?"

I nodded.

"Great." Owen held the door open for me, and Taco and I went with him into the interrogation room.

"Good morning," I said to Victoria.

She didn't answer as she looked up at me, fear written in her eyes. I wondered if she really had something to worry about. I guessed we'd find out.

"Hi there," Owen said, sitting down next to me and greeting Victoria. His easy smile and affable manner put most people at ease, and she did not seem immune to his charms. Her shoulders lowered slightly.

"Hi."

"Thanks for coming in this morning. We just had a few quick questions to ask you about your evening meeting with Camille Hawthorne at the Paw Spa the other night, and then we'll let you be on your way."

I marveled at how Owen had slipped in the assumption that Victoria not only went to the Paw Spa, but that she met with Camille there.

Victoria's mouth dropped into a little o shape, but she didn't deny the statement.

Owen nodded to himself, glancing at his notes. "So you arrived at the spa just after nine in the evening," he said. "Is that right?"

Victoria's eyes darted between us. "I suppose. It isn't like I made an appointment in my calendar or anything. It was dark, though. Pretty late."

"And why did you go there that night?"

I knew Victoria was considering whether to stick to her

story—that she'd forgotten something there earlier—or to admit that she was there for some other reason.

"Camille and I had something to discuss."

I was happy to hear her tell the truth.

"So Camille asked you to meet her there?" Owen asked.

Victoria fidgeted with her hands in her lap, and then squared her shoulders and looked up at us. "No. I asked her to meet me there."

More truth. That was good.

"What did you hope to discuss with Camille?" Owen asked.

Victoria sighed. "I wanted to ask her again to stop spreading lies about me. About my dogs."

"Tell us about those," I suggested.

Victoria rolled her eyes. "It's gone on forever. Always the same stories. I wanted her to drop her insistence that BoBo Jingles wasn't a proper champion. He has all the documentation and he's been a stud to several litters, all of which have produced champions. It's been years, and I've had enough of her lies damaging my reputation and my business. I was going to appeal to her humanity, try to make her see how damaging her words were..."

"And how did Camille respond to your request?" Owen asked, leaning in.

Shaking her head, Victoria sighed. "I never got to ask her at all."

"Why not?" I asked.

"When I got there, Camille was there, in a total panic. Her dog had been put in a kennel to stay overnight, and he was gone. She was freaking out, storming around and looking for him."

"So the dognapping had already happened," I said, mostly to Owen. Given the order of the comings and goings that night, it was clear that Marla Carver was the dognapper.

"I guess so. Beau wasn't at the Paw Spa, and Camille was hysterical," Victoria said.

"And no one else was inside?" I asked.

Victoria practically snapped her answer. "No. Just me and Camille."

"So what happened?" Owen asked.

Victoria crossed her arms over her chest. "She blamed me for Beau's absence, of course. Said I was the kind of person who would steal her champion dog because I couldn't seem to breed one of my own."

"That probably hurt," Owen suggested.

One of Victoria's shoulders lifted, and she made a humming sound of assent. "I guess."

"What did you do next?"

"I tried to talk with her, but she was so furious, she was practically unintelligible. I left."

"That was all? You went in, you found Beau missing and Camille upset. You argued and then you left."

Victoria nodded, but then tilted her head to one side. "I didn't say we argued."

"Did you argue?" Owen asked.

She hesitated. "A little bit."

"And I think I know the answer, but just to confirm, Camille Hawthorne was alive when you left."

A frown creased Victoria's forehead, and she said, "Of course. I didn't even touch her." Her voice rose to an unnaturally high pitch on this last statement.

Owen made a few notes in his phone and then pushed it into his pocket. He glanced at me, an eyebrow raised, and I knew he was asking if I had any more questions. I shook my head.

"Victoria, thank you again for coming in. I trust that you'll be available if we have any further questions."

"Sure." Victoria's usual composure had disappeared and she looked very near to tears.

"Thank you. You're free to go. I'll walk you out."

When Owen returned from seeing Victoria to the exit, we settled in his office.

"It seems like Victoria was the last person to see Camille alive," he said.

"Or the first to see her not alive," I pointed out.

He nodded, his eyes narrowing as he seemed to consider something. "Did she seem like there was something she wasn't telling us, maybe?"

"Maybe. Or she's not telling the entire truth? She was

nervous, but the way she avoided coming in for as long as possible makes me think she has something to hide."

"Exactly," Owen said.

We both sat in thought for a moment, and then I remembered that he'd mentioned Elliott Nazar when I'd first arrived. "Did you have news about Elliott?"

"I've located him, and he should be coming in for questioning today or tomorrow."

I nodded. "Great."

"In the meantime," Owen said. "We've received permission to search Camille Hawthorne's summer residence. Care to join me?"

"Definitely."

Within the hour we were pulling up to a house nestled into the hillside above Saltcliff, where we were met by Camille's housekeeper, Marva.

"I called ahead, but we have a warrant if she wants to see it," Owen told me as we exited the car.

Marva waited at the bottom of the outdoor steps, wringing her hands. I wondered how long she'd been standing there.

"Hello," she said, looking between us and down to Taco. "I'm happy to show you around, or just let you wander. As long as it helps find out who did this to poor Camille."

As we headed to the front door, Owen asked, "have you known Camille long?"

Marva nodded. "Most of my life. We grew up together. When Camille's husband died, she asked if I would like to move in."

Owen and I exchanged a glance.

"We'd been best friends as children, you see. But life took us in very different directions. I married a Marine, raised my family, and then was left on my own when he died. Camille married a wealthy man but was left alone too. We came back together in our old age," she said, almost wistfully.

We stepped into the entry of a modest but well-appointed home with light streaming in from a collection of high windows.

"You're friends," Owen said, glancing around. "And yet, you work for her?"

Marva lifted a shoulder. "I'm not good at sitting idle, and I had no real income. I didn't like the idea of living here without making some kind of contribution."

I nodded. That made sense to me.

"And when was the last time you saw Camille?" Owen asked.

Marva's eyes filled with tears. "The night she disappeared. The night she was... killed. I broke a glass in the kitchen, and she became upset because I wasn't able to be sure I'd found every single sliver. With the show coming up, she didn't want to risk Beaumont injuring a paw, so she took him to the Paw Spa to stay, then came home to help me clean."

"Camille helped you clean?" I couldn't help the question—it seemed so contrary to the character we'd gotten to know.

"Yes," Marva said, looking between us. "She wasn't as hoity-toity as she wanted everyone to believe. That was just her public persona. She was a complicated woman. But we were friends."

"Go on," Owen suggested.

"She came back, we cleaned and ate dinner, and then she told me she was going to go check on Beau and left. I never saw either one of them again."

"Beau will be returned to you today," Owen assured her, and Marva smiled widely. "And what did you do for the rest of the evening while Camille was out?"

"I talked with my sister on the phone for a bit and went to bed around ten."

Owen collected Marva's sister's information and then thanked her for answering questions.

"One more. Did Camille have an office? Somewhere she kept important documents?" He asked.

"Through here." Marva led us to a room off the main living area, which was furnished like a library with tall shelves containing books and even featuring a rolling ladder to reach the highest shelves. There was a feminine desk positioned at one end with an enormous potted plant next to it and a pink upholstered chair on wheels behind it.

"Thank you," Owen said, moving to the desk.

We spent an hour going through the files Camille kept in her drawer, and looking through various other odds and ends, without turning up much of interest. Finally, Owen felt around under the desk and pulled the drawers all the way.

"What are you doing?" I asked.

"Looking for a hiding spot." As he said this, he grinned at me and popped the bottom out of one of the drawers, revealing a hidden space beneath it. A false bottom. Inside, there was a little red book. Owen pulled it out and flipped through it.

"Dahlia, look." The pages were tagged with tape flags bearing peoples' names.

"Victoria Dane. Marla Carver. Elliott Nazar. Nina Reyes. And so many more," I whispered. "What is this?"

Owen flipped to Victoria Dane's name. "Breeding practices suspect," he read. "BoBo Jingles not from a champion line. See Harley Smith."

"Who is Harley Smith?" I asked.

Owen flipped to the page tagged with that name. "Provides fake documents for cash." He raised an eyebrow as he looked at me. "Camille has dirt on just about everyone."

"Am I in there?" I asked, curiosity getting the better of me.

Owen flipped through the pages again. "No, and neither am I. Marva has a page, though. Most folks around town do, it looks like. It's gonna take a while to process this little book of secrets." He slipped it into a plastic bag and tucked it into his pocket.

We spent another hour looking through the house, but didn't find anything else that seemed relevant. Once we thanked Marva, we headed out. As we pulled up to the station, Owen said, "I have one more question for Nina Reyes. Feel like a walk to the Paw Spa?"

"Sure," I said. Taco was already on his feet at the word "walk."

We made our way through town and arrived to find the Paw Spa quite busy, which made sense since the show was in two days. Nina's eyes found us the second the bell over the door sounded, and her expression said that she was not pleased to see us.

"What now?" she asked, calling to us from the hydrotherapy tub in the back room where she was washing another big dog. This one looked like some kind of sheepdog.

We headed that way, and crowded into the little space. Taco and I moved to the corner, where the metal stool was shoved against the wall. Owen spoke with Nina in quiet tones as my dog sniffed around with interest.

"I just wondered if you have a key to the back door," Owen said, keeping his voice friendly.

Nina glanced between us and then said, "Of course I do. This is my business."

Owen nodded as Taco tugged uncharacteristically at his leash, pulling me closer to the wall.

"Taco, stop," I said quietly, though it did little good.

"Do you ever come and go through that door?" Owen asked.

Nina didn't answer for a moment, and I glanced to where Taco continued to pull, nosing around the edge of the metal stool. I moved to where his focus was, surprised to find a dark mark smeared along one corner of the stool's top. It was almost black, but not quite, and it was flaking off at one edge like paint. Or blood.

"Owen," I said softly, forgetting that he was in the midst of asking Nina a question.

"Nina," he repeated. "Do you ever use the back door instead of the front? To come in or to leave for the day?"

I glanced up to see Nina shrug. "Sometimes, I guess. I get deliveries that way and sometimes come in there to bring them in with me."

Owen nodded. "Okay, thanks." He moved to where I knelt by the stool. Taco had relaxed now, and sat at my side as if happy that I'd finally noticed what he was trying to show me.

"Is this blood?" I asked Owen.

He peered down at it, frowning. "It definitely looks like it." He pulled a pair of gloves and a plastic bag from his pocket, and then flaked a bit of the substance into the bag.

"You always carry that around?" I asked him.

He grinned. "Like a Boy Scout."

"Do Boy Scouts carry latex gloves?" I didn't think I knew that.

Owen laughed. "Maybe, but I know that they are always prepared."

"Oh. Yes, that makes sense," I agreed. Then I realized that I'd misunderstood yet another joke and the flush began to climb my cheeks.

The smile Owen flashed at me immediately made me smile back. He liked that I didn't always get the joke. And he wasn't judging me for it.

"If that's all," Nina said, "I'm pretty busy in here today as you can see."

"Of course," Owen said. "We'll get out of the way."

We left the Paw Spa through the back door and Owen peered at the lock with a frown. "Nina might have a key, but someone who wanted in at some point didn't," he said.

I leaned over and peered at the lock. "What do you mean?"

"See these scratches?" Owen pointed to the scratched face of the deadbolt lock, which bore tiny striations and a couple deeper dents.

"Yes."

"Someone has picked this lock," he said.

"Think it has something to do with Camille?" I asked.

He shrugged. "Maybe, maybe not. The scratches look fairly new, but there's really no way to tell."

"Hey Owen?" I began, thinking. "Would picking a lock damage it?"

He straightened and looked at me. "It could. Very experienced lock pickers can generally open locks without any damage, but someone with less skill or a really tricky lock can end up damaged or even ruined."

"Nina told us that the lock has been acting weird lately when she opened it."

"Interesting. I'll dig into that. Good job spotting that blood. I'll get it to the lab," he said.

"Think it's Camille's?" I asked.

"That's what we need to find out," he said.

When we left the spa, we went our separate ways. I had a full house at the inn, and spent the remainder of the day helping tidy the rooms, chatting with guests and directing them to things around town, and preparing for breakfast the following morning.

I had never seen so many dogs in Saltcliff, and it was a very dog-friendly town. There were dogs everywhere you looked on the sidewalk, walking, trotting, galloping. Dogs crowded the little green park near the library in the center of town, and they also populated the front garden and back lawn of the Saltcliff B&B. It made me happy, but it also added an element of chaos that had a slightly unsettling effect on me despite my best efforts. The dogs also made keeping the inn tidy a bit more of a chore, given the vast amounts of dog fur being deposited in the rugs, on the arms of the furniture, and even in the bedclothes.

"I've never seen this kind of volume come out of the dryer screen," Amal exclaimed as she changed a load of sheets and held up a thick handful of dog hair and lint from cleaning the screen.

"I supposed we should be happy that our dryer seems to be very efficient," I said.

"We might need to look at having the ducts cleaned when this is all over," she said.

"Did the dog show people not stay here last year?" I had assumed this was an annual takeover and that Daisy must have had to handle it just as we were now.

"No, they stayed at lots of other places, but we never had a full house like this. Come to think of it, we've been much busier in recent months than we ever have been before."

I frowned, thinking. "Why would that be true?"

Amal smiled at me and caught my eyes. "I think, Dahlia, you might need to consider that you are actually a very good innkeeper."

I enjoyed the praise, of course. But hadn't my sister been a good innkeeper? I wanted to say something — I knew how close Amal and Daisy had been. Before I could think of what to say, Amal spoke again.

"Dahlia, your sister was an amazing person. But she wasn't detail oriented. And the breakfasts she put out were nothing in comparison. It seems word has spread."

"Oh. Well." I fastened my gaze on my hands. "Thank you."

Amal squeezed one of my hands and then hurried off. I loaded the washing machine and set it running, and then returned upstairs to the lobby where Taco was curled on his bed and Amal was already handling a line of guests with questions at the front desk.

Late that afternoon, things calmed down as guests left for dinner plans out in town, and I checked in with Diantha, who was busily watching dog show videos and trying to decide what to wear when she and Taco took their turn in the arena.

"A skirt?" she said, facing me and rubbing a finger across her cheek in a thoughtful manner. "Or slacks?"

"Danny, do you even own anything you'd call 'slacks'?" When I met my niece, she had favored ripped jeans and black tights. Now her palette was more colorful, and she wore far less dark makeup, but I still didn't think she had anything that would be mistaken for business attire.

"No, maybe not," she said. "So what should I wear?" Her voice had an edge of distress, and I sensed that this was one of those moments when Daisy would have had just the right thing to say or do.

"Let's look at the options," I said. "But you know very well that fashion is not my forté."

"I know," she said with a sigh.

She pulled out several pairs of pants and a few blouses with buttons and flowers, and made a few different outfits on her bed.

"This one is very nice," I said, pointing to a pair of khaki pants with a pink and blue floral blouse.

"Mom bought me that blouse to wear one Easter," she said. "I don't think I've worn it since then." She pulled it on over the tight T-shirt she wore, only to find that the buttons did not meet in the middle. "Oh no."

"Wait," I said, having an idea. "Let it hang open for a moment."

She stopped trying to pull it closed and let it hang open over the T-shirt. "Oh."

"If you wore it like that over a tank top, maybe?"

She smiled. "Aunt Dolly, that's a great idea."

"And maybe the denim skirt?" I didn't think anyone would expect to see a twelve-year old dressing like a fifty-year-old, and this seemed appropriate.

"Thanks," she said, giving me a quick hug as I turned to head to the kitchen to bake.

I was just getting out ingredients when Owen texted.

Owen: The blood on the stool is Camille's.

Oh. Well.

Me: So... that means...

Owen: I think it means that there may have been some kind of attack in the Paw Spa. If Camille hit her head on that stool, she would have ended up on the floor—not in the tub. Someone had to put her in the tub.

Me: Right... So maybe she was so distressed at finding Beau gone that she tripped and hit her head?

Owen: Maybe. Let's sleep on this. I'll chat with you in the morning.

Me: Okay.

I went to bed soon after, but couldn't sleep. My mind was busy trying to figure out how Camille had ended up in the tub.

Chapter Thirteen

The day before the Saltcliff Dog Show, it felt like the whole town of Saltcliff had taken on a completely different atmosphere. Besides the extreme focus on canines, there was a vibration in the air, a "vibe," as my niece would call it. It was frenetic and excited, and frankly, it made me a bit nervous.

Normally, I'd take Taco out for a long walk to clear my head, but that wasn't an option since there were literally dogs everywhere, and he was picking up on the excitement just as I was. I attended to breakfast and helped Amal turn over rooms as needed, but since most guests were staying over, there were only a few requesting housekeeping and new towels. As the breakfast rush passed, I slipped down to the not-yet-open speakeasy for a bit of quiet.

Once there, I outlined everything we knew about

Camille Hawthorne's death, and the things we still didn't know.

There was the blood on the stool, which made me think maybe it had just been an accident, except that it would have been impossible for Camille to hit her head on the stool and then fall into the tub.

So it was likely not an accident at all.

Then there was the strange man who'd arrived at the Paw Spa that night but not entered. Could it have been Elliott Nazar? Or someone we didn't even know about? But why would he change his mind? Did he see something that made him change his mind about going in?

And then there was Victoria Dane. And Marla Carver. It was possible all three of the women had been inside the Paw Spa at once. Had Victoria and Marla worked together? They both had reasons to be angry with Camille, who seemed to be quite adept at blackmail and who clearly had dirt on everyone.

It was possible that either Marla or Victoria knew how Camille had ended up with the head wound, but neither woman had given any information to indicate that knowledge.

I was deep in thought when my cell phone chimed with a new text.

Owen: Can you join me at the station? Victoria Dane is here.

I jumped to my feet and typed a quick response and then headed to meet Owen at the station.

"She's in room one," Owen said, coming to meet me in the lobby of the police station. "And she's in quite a state."

"What kind of state?"

"You'll see," he said.

The state Owen referred to was one of distress. Victoria, normally impeccably put together and refined, was lying over her arms, slumped on the table in tears when we entered. She lifted her head and looked between Owen and me before dissolving into tears once again.

"I'm so sorry," she wailed. "I didn't mean to do it. I didn't know she was dead. I barely touched her!"

I exchanged a quick glance with Owen, who started his recorder.

"Victoria, can you please repeat everything you told me for Dahlia."

The woman's back heaved and she raised her head once again. I could see the struggle she went through to try to pull herself together to speak. She let out a shuddering breath and blew her nose into a tissue before she appeared able to speak.

Owen and I sat across from her.

"I did it," she declared, looking right at me. "I didn't mean to, but I killed Camille Hawthorne."

Oh. Well. A confession was the last thing I'd expected. It certainly did make things easier, though.

"You did?" I asked, thinking through everything she'd told us before.

She nodded miserably, her tears pulling lines of black makeup down her cheeks. "She met me there, and like I said, she was upset. But I didn't care. I demanded she stop spreading lies about me. She was furious and distraught over Beau. And we argued for a few minutes in the kennel area, and then she stormed into the grooming room. She was shouting at me and wouldn't listen to a word of reason. When she grabbed my arm and shook me, I couldn't help it —I reacted."

Victoria quieted then, and I waited. She took a deep breath and went on.

"I fought back."

She said nothing else, and I glanced at Owen.

"Go on," he said. "Please describe what happened next."

Victoria looked about to crumble again, but she pushed her shoulders back and continued. "We kind of...wrestled, I guess. She grabbed my arm and I pushed her off, and she flew at me, slapping and hitting. I kicked her, I think, and then I shoved her, hard." Victoria sniffed and blew her nose again as we waited. "She went over backwards. It all happened really fast, and I just... I thought she'd get up."

"So she went over backwards and fell to the floor?" Owen asked.

Victoria nodded.

"Did she hit her head?"

"I don't know, it was so fast, and I was so upset. I guess she must have. There was a metal stool there. So maybe."

"So she didn't get back up?" I asked.

"N-no. She just laid there, on the floor of the grooming room. I didn't know what to do."

"What did you do?" Owen asked, his voice gentle.

Victoria dropped her gaze to her hands. "I checked to make sure she was breathing. And she was. She was just... unconscious, I guess. And then I left. I thought she'd wake up, and I didn't want to fight with her again. I realized how stupid it had been to confront her—women like Camille never listen to reason." She shook her head. "I just... I had no idea she was dying. That I'd... I'd killed her..." She broke down again, crumpling over her arms and shaking.

I stared at her and then turned to Owen, who nodded toward the door.

"Victoria, we're going to step out and get you some water, okay?"

She sniffled miserably, but didn't answer as we left the room.

In the vestibule, I turned to Owen. "What do you think?"

He shook his head. "She didn't kill Camille."

"She doesn't know Camille drowned."

"We haven't made that public knowledge. Only a few

of us know that's how she died. But this would explain the gash on her head. And the blood."

"But the blood is next to the tub, not in the grooming room," I pointed out.

Owen rubbed a hand over his jaw. "We need to examine the grooming room more closely. I suspect we'll find traces there too. And I think now we can hypothesize that someone else found Camille unconscious and moved her."

"Or that Victoria isn't telling the whole truth."

"She just confessed to murder. I'm willing to bet she thinks it's the whole truth."

I nodded at that. If someone was willing to confess to murder, they probably wouldn't change the means by which they committed it.

I stared at Owen. "What now?"

He sighed. "I would like to talk to Derek a little more, and we still need to get Elliott here. I also have a few more questions for Marla, but she's been very evasive since we last questioned her."

"Okay. Do you think Derek is hiding something?"

"Could be. I'd like to know if he had a key to the back door."

"Or lock picking skills," I said, meaning for it be a joke.

Owen looked at me thoughtfully. "Good point." He was quiet another second. "Do you suppose Taco might be able to sniff out more of Camille's blood if there is any in the grooming room?"

I thought about that. "I think he probably could. He found the first bit."

"I had John out front call Nina this morning. The Paw Spa is once again considered an active crime scene, so it's shut down. I just hope we haven't compromised it too much by letting her reopen so quickly."

"I'm sure Nina isn't happy about that." I thought of all the dog show patrons who would be going elsewhere.

"No, she's not. Add her to the list."

"Who else is unhappy?"

"Marla has been served with fines for operating the Regal Retreat without a proper business license. She's shut down too, until the inspection takes place."

I raised my eyebrows. That wasn't something he'd mentioned before.

Owen smiled. "Marla is being rather uncooperative. I thought this might make her more likely to come in and chat."

I nodded. "Where is Beau now?"

"Back with Marva at Camille's."

"Do you think she'll press charges?" I asked.

Owen nodded. "Dog theft. John's spoken with her about it."

I sighed. Camille Hawthorne had not been very well-liked. I felt glad there was someone who had been on her side. "So I'll take Taco to the spa, you chat with Derek."

"Right."

"And Owen?"

Owen smiled at me. "Yes?"

"Tomorrow I'll need to be off to support Danny and Taco at the show."

"We'll both be there," he said. "I wouldn't miss it. Plus, we may learn something there."

"I'll talk to you soon," I said.

Owen leaned down and kissed my cheek, and I went back to the hotel to gather Taco to do some investigating.

Taco and Diantha were in the back yard at the inn, practicing their tricks for the show the next day.

"Aunt Dolly, watch!" Diantha led Taco through five separate tricks, ending with him sitting up on his hind legs and grinning at me.

I clapped enthusiastically. "Amazing! You guys have made so much progress in so little time. It's really astounding."

Diantha hugged my dog, who looked exceptionally

proud of himself. "Now I think we just need to rest up for the big day. You're going to go with us tomorrow, right?"

I nodded. "I already spoke to Owen. We'll have to suspend the investigation for a day."

We went into the inn, and I told Diantha about Owen's idea to take Taco back to the Paw Spa.

"Can I come?"

I frowned, feeling like my young niece had already been a bit too involved in a murder investigation, but Diantha's expression was very difficult to refuse.

"I suppose, since you're essentially his handler at this point," I said.

A half hour later we were at the Paw Spa, having been let in by the police guard stationed at the door.

"You have your own police ID now? That's awesome," Diantha said, grinning at me. My ID had not gotten us entry, however. The guard had still called Owen to confirm. Not that I really minded.

Inside, we stood for a moment just beyond the door. It was strange to see the place quiet and empty, since almost every time I'd been here, it had been quite busy.

"So we are looking to see if there's blood anywhere else here, right?" Diantha asked.

"Yes," I said. "Specifically in the grooming area, and if there are any traces leading into the room with the big hydrotherapy tub there." I pointed the path I imagined

Camille's body might have taken to get from the grooming room to the tub.

"Okay," Diantha said. "Let's start back here." She led Taco to the hydrotherapy tub where I'd told her we had discovered the blood before. I looked for the metal stool, but it did not seem to be in the room. A quick check of the grooming room confirmed that it had been moved. If the stool was used in both spaces, then Victoria could have been right about Camille hitting her head on it as she fell in the grooming room.

"We found blood before on this stool," I told Diantha, leading her back to where the stool now sat. Diantha let Taco sniff around it. The blood had been cleaned off, but I hoped he might still have a scent to follow.

"Find it, Taco!" Diantha said, dropping his leash and letting my dog wander on his own. Taco lowered his nose and poked around the edges of the grooming room before moving to sniff the threshold to the room. Diantha and I moved out of his way as he sniffed through the main space and then followed his nose to the doorway that opened into the hydrotherapy room.

He paused, sniffing just inside the door and barked once.

"Aunt Dolly, look!" Diantha rushed to see what Taco was interested in and pointed out a vague dark smear on the beige tile. "Find it, Taco!" Diantha told him again, and Taco resumed work, heading back into the grooming room.

He circled the tables, and paused beneath one, alerting again.

There was another light smear next to the leg of one of the tables. It looked like it had been scrubbed almost clean, but not quite.

"Good boy, Taco," I told him, giving his velvety ears a good rub.

"Why is there blood all over the place?" Diantha asked, looking worried.

"I'm not sure," I told her. "But I think it means that poor Camille didn't just hit her head on the stool and fall into the tub. I think it means she was hurt in here and then someone moved her."

My niece's eyebrows rose and she repeated me. "That poor lady."

We left the spa after telling the officer outside what we'd found and showing him the marks. He said he would call for a team to come gather the evidence. I called Owen as we walked back to the Inn.

"Good work Taco," he said with a smile in his voice. "I had a chat with Derek, too. And with his mother."

Derek was only seventeen, so I was glad to hear his mother was with him.

"He does have a key to the back door of the spa, which complicates things a bit."

"So he might have come and gone without us seeing."

"I don't think he did, though. He stopped by that night because he'd forgotten his AirPods in the grooming room."

"But we didn't see him go in." I thought back to the list of people Owen had seen on the footage.

"No, but we did see a man approach the door with a key and then turn away."

"Ah... Derek?"

"Sounds like it. He admitted that he'd gotten to the door and seen a foot on the ground coming out of the grooming room."

"Camille's."

"He was scared. He went home and told his mother."

"What did she do?"

Owen sighed. "Nothing. She said he was prone to exaggeration and that she was busy."

Wow. "Okay. Poor Derek." I felt sorry for any kid whose parents assumed they weren't telling the truth.

"He said he wasn't really sure what he saw. He thought maybe she was right, and he was overreacting, or that Nina had just left a pair of shoes inside."

"But he was sure enough not to want to go back and get his AirPods," I pointed out.

"True," Owen agreed.

"And then when he came back in the morning, he found her in the tub," I said, thinking aloud.

"Right. So he still isn't sure if he saw what he thought he saw the night before."

"So where does that leave us?" I asked.

"I'm still trying to reach Elliott, and we need to get the lab to look at the samples you just found. We should be ready to draw some conclusions by tomorrow, I think."

I nodded, though Owen couldn't see me. "So... we think this was... "

"I'm not going to guess, but I think we're on the same page, Dahlia."

I wasn't quite sure what page I was on. The person with the most access was Nina, plus there was the potential that Camille was blackmailing her... but we still didn't know why. And if blackmail was the motive, the little book we'd found implicated many more people. Camille had dirt on everyone. And without knowing exactly what she had on Nina, it was impossible to know if Nina would be desperate enough to kill her.

Diantha and I returned to the inn to find it busier than ever. Amal was running to and fro, answering guest concerns, and I felt guilty for having been so distracted during our busiest time yet.

Even Diantha was put to work helping collect dishes from the lobby and common areas, and loading the dishwasher in the laundry room.

By the time the evening had quieted down, and I invited Amal in for a cup of tea while I pulled together the morning's baked goods, we were all exhausted.

"I'm going to bed early," Diantha announced, standing

in the doorway to the kitchen as Amal sat at the round table. "Need to be well rested for the show."

"Good luck tomorrow, Danny. I can't wait to watch." Amal smiled at her.

The inn was going to be closed for services during the dog show the following day. Guests had keys to the front and their rooms, so they could come and go, but I'd had a sign up all week that there would be no one manning the desk until after the dog show.

"I can't wait," Diantha squealed and then turned on her heel and headed off to bed.

"She's so excited," Amal said with a sigh.

"She is," I agreed, setting her tea steaming before her. "How are you?"

"I'm excited for her," she said.

"I don't mean about the dog show. How are things with your family? Have you decided to go home?"

Amal shook her head lightly. "I still really don't know. It would be an uncomfortable trip—both in terms of a very long flight and also many unresolved family issues. I'm just not sure I'm up for it."

I nodded. That did make sense. But it didn't feel right to me. I measured flour into a bowl for the muffin mix I was making as I contemplated how to articulate what I was thinking.

"I know it might be difficult to be home," I said. "To have some of the conversations you're dreading."

"It will." Amal sounded certain.

"But there will come a point where the people who need to have those conversations might not be able to have them."

Amal cocked her head to one side as I turned back to look at her.

"People age. They become less functional. They..."

"They die."

"They do." I thought of my sister, of the unresolved issues between us. "I can only speak from my own experience. But I regret the time I let pass without trying to understand the issues facing Daisy and me."

"I know."

"I feel like it would have been the right thing to make the effort, even if she didn't want to talk to me. To see me."

"She did want to see you. But she had the same fears as you."

"Fears?" That got my attention.

"Rejection. Anger. Being pushed away or unloved."

I added the sugar to the bowl in front of me, and then turned to face my friend. "Aren't those the same fears you have?"

"The exact ones." She sighed and sipped her tea. "I just can't imagine going all the way there to try to make things right and then ending up feeling like it was all wasted time, like nothing will change even though I tried."

"But you would know that you tried."

Amal gave a half smile and a little shrug. "I don't know if that's worth it."

I wondered if it was. "It seems like it would be better to know you did all you could than to wonder what might have happened..."

"Maybe," she said, her voice soft.

"When do you need to decide?" I asked.

"Within the next week. The wedding is in May."

I mixed the dry ingredients with a big whisk and then went to the table to sip my own tea. "It's a hard decision."

"It is," Amal agreed. "Thanks for the support."

Chapter Fourteen

The inn was abuzz the next morning, and most owners and pets were out early, heading down to the convention center where the show would be held. Diantha, Taco, and I left as many of the guests did, and Amal promised to lock up and meet us just before the show was scheduled to start. As a participant, Taco was expected to arrive early enough to locate our ring, make sure we understood the schedule, and do a bit of last-minute grooming to make sure he looked his best.

"This is so exciting!" Diantha said, as we made our way between the dogs being groomed one last time in the preparation area. We found our ring and the area where we were to wait, and settled in.

"There are so many dogs here," I noted, feeling immediately silly for stating the obvious.

"It is a dog show," Diantha laughed.

Taco, for his part, panted away happily, gazing around him at the hustle and bustle going on in every corner of the preparation area. Diantha busied herself brushing his fur out carefully and making last minute trims to the fur between his toes. Taco seemed more than happy to allow her ministrations. Any attention was good attention.

I wandered around a little bit, meandering through the preparation areas for some of the other groups of dogs. As I passed two handlers chatting, I paused as I heard a few snippets of their conversation.

"But some people go too far," one woman said. "You remember the groomer who started that scandal with the schnauzer?"

"Oh yes! She misgroomed him on purpose, right?"

I cringed at the thought of hurting a dog, I hoped that wasn't what had happened.

"Yep. Trimmed his moustache crooked, and he couldn't show. They never proved the why behind it, I don't think, but it sounded like someone was paying her to do it."

"She left show grooming, I hope. What was her name again?"

I inspected my fingernails as I lingered nearby, pretending to be disinterested.

"I don't remember... but she definitely left. Tail between her legs!"

"I should hope. She was young too, wasn't she?"

The second woman laughed. "Future ruined. Sheesh."

There seemed to be a lot of dirty dealings in the world of dog showing—who knew? The only dog groomer I knew was Nina, and though she'd been busier at the Paw Spa in the days leading up to the show, she wasn't here in any official capacity as a groomer. But that would certainly be a truth she would want to keep quiet... still, the odds it was Nina they'd been discussing were slim. Weren't they?

I hurried back to Diantha.

"Taco's on in a minute," she said, bouncing on her toes. "Amal just texted. She has seats in the third row."

"Okay," I said, putting aside the case for a moment. "I'll go sit with her. Good luck, Danny! Do great, Taco Dog!" I kissed my dog's wet snout and hurried out to the stands where Owen and Amal sat together overlooking the ring.

"And now," cried the announcer over the speaker. "We welcome our local dogs for several competitions including skills, agility, and the popular all-around best dog."

As he finished speaking, twelve groups of dogs and owners strode out into the ring, Diantha third among them smiling broadly with Taco at her side. They stopped in their designated spot and Taco sat immediately, looking relaxed and happy.

"They look great," Owen said, taking my hand and giving it a squeeze.

I held his hand tightly. "Why am I nervous?" I asked. I was only watching.

"Me too," Amal laughed.

The host introduced all the dogs and their handlers, and we clapped and cheered when he announced Taco Dog and Diantha. Then, each dog was brought to the middle of the ring to show off their skills.

A tiny chihuahua refused to cooperate, running away from his owner and diving to the ground for a good roll before she got hold of him again. A golden retriever did some impressive tricks for his handler, and I wondered if he might have a leg up on Taco and Diantha.

But when it was Taco's turn, he put on a fantastic show, playing to the crowd, which adored him. He grinned out at those clapping and cheering after each trick, and looked like he'd been performing for an audience all his life.

The agility dogs were taken to a side ring to run through an obstacle course, and I thought that was very interesting. Taco could probably do that, but the Australian Shepherd was by far the fastest at completing the course.

"We'll now have our judges come out to meet each of the dogs."

One by one, the dogs were examined by three judges, who felt their fur and paws, looked into their mouths and lifted their tails.

"That's a bit personal," Owen said as Taco's tail was examined.

Finally, we came to the part where the judges invited their three winners to the center of the ring. A woman in a royal blue skirt walked around the waiting pairs and selected the Aussie, the golden retriever, and Taco Dog.

We cheered as Diantha and my dog moved to the center of the ring.

"First, the agility winner, Harry and his handler, Seth Adams!" The man with the Australian shepherd beamed.

"Next, our skills winner, Rufus and his handler Sissy Green!" The golden retriever.

"Finally, our all-around best dog, Taco Dog and his handler Danny Vale!"

I was on my feet cheering before I'd even made a decision to get up. Amal and Owen were standing too, all three of us clapping excitedly for Diantha and Taco.

Diantha was handed a trophy, and the judge placed a ribbon around Taco's neck, and they made a quick circle of the ring before exiting.

"Let's go find them," Amal said, and we hurried back to the prep area to congratulate my niece.

When we arrived at the prep area, Diantha and Taco were surrounded by excited well-wishers, Lou Grant among them.

"Hello again," I said, stepping up next to him.

"Hi Dahlia. Did you get to the bottom of the dognapping case?"

"We did," I said. "I'm sorry to have dragged you into it."

"Well, you didn't. Marla dragged me into it, I guess."

I nodded. "You really think her framing you was just a case of sour grapes?"

He shook his head. "Guess maybe I was just a convenient target, since she probably thought I was still close to Camille and Beau."

"Right. She wouldn't know you'd been let go. And maybe when she heard Camille was dead, she realized how shady everything looked. She panicked."

"Is that what she told you?" Lou tilted his head, eyeing me.

"No... just a guess."

He nodded, and seemed about to take his leave when something occurred to me. "Lou?"

"Yeah?"

"You've been on the show circuit a long time, haven't you?"

"You could say that." He crossed his meaty arms and settled back on his heels as if preparing for a challenge.

"Ever hear about a show groomer misgrooming a dog on purpose so it couldn't compete?"

"You talking about Santa Fe? The schnauzer?" His

eyebrow rose and he chuckled. "That was years ago. I hadn't even put it together. Think it's something?"

I tilted my head, unsure what he meant. "Do I think what is something?"

"Oh, I figured you'd lined that all up. It was Nina. The groomer. She cut a schnauzer's mustache incorrectly back in Santa Fe almost a decade ago, disqualifying him for departing from the breed standard cut. The owner found out it wasn't an accident. She was paid to disqualify him so another dog could win."

I thought about that. Could that have been the thing Camille was holding over her head? "Did many people know?"

He shook his head. "I don't think so. It was kept pretty hush hush on the condition Nina left show grooming altogether."

Lou had worked closely with Camille. "Did Camille Hawthorne know?"

"Of course she did. She had dirt on everyone."

"Was it Beau who benefitted?" I asked.

"Oh no. It was another schnauzer, but I'm not sure Camille was above that kind of thing when it suited her."

That Camille had dirt on everyone was certainly true, but this was the dirt we'd been looking for. Camille's little book of names and secrets was practically written in code. All it said under Nina's name was "Santa Fe." Now it made sense. I glanced around for Owen. He was busily chatting with Diantha and Amal, who were still surrounded by a crowd.

"I'm gonna head out to watch the next few rounds," Lou said. "Got a couple leads on some new work."

"That's great," I said, waving as he walked away.

Chapter Fifteen

The Saltcliff police were busier the evening after the dog show than they'd probably been in months. After telling Owen what I'd learned about Nina's past, he ordered her brought in, and decided to issue a warrant for Marla as well, since she still refused to come in on her own. A warrant had also been put out for Elliott Nazar, who remained impossible to find.

Both women were kept in holding cells overnight, which I imagined was most unpleasant, and Owen and I met at the station early the following morning. I let Taco Dog rest at the Inn. He'd had a big week, after all.

"I think we're about to wrap this up, Dahlia," he said, handing me a steaming cup of green tea. He knew it was my drink of choice, and must have stopped by Valerie's especially to pick it up. The knowledge sent a little tingle of gratitude through me.

"Thanks for the tea."

Owen smiled at me and something in his eyes warmed my insides more than the tea did.

"So who do we talk to first?" I asked.

"Marla, I think. Room two."

I nodded, still a little uncomfortable in these official interviews. I wasn't a police officer, after all.

We headed into the interrogation room, and Owen handed Marla a paper cup of coffee.

"Sleep okay?" he asked as he sat.

Marla scowled at him and then turned her furious gaze on me. "Keeping me in jail overnight seems a bit excessive," she spat.

"I called and stopped by several times, but you were unavailable. We're trying to wrap up an active investigation. I'm sure you understand."

"I do not." She was furious, and part of me didn't blame her. "I already told you everything, paid the license fees to reopen the Regal Retreat, and received notice I'm being charged with dog theft. What more do you need?"

"All we need is your version of how the champion Borzoi Beaumont Royale came to be at your establishment the day we found him there," Owen said, setting his recorder on the table.

Marla sniffed, lifting her chin. "I have told you everything already!"

"You've given us one version. We're ready for what really happened."

She looked between us, and then seemed to make a decision, deflating slightly. "Fine." She took a sip of the coffee, made a face, and then leaned back in her chair. "I went to the Paw Spa, used my code, and took Beau out the back."

Owen nodded encouragingly. "Why do you have a code to the Paw Spa?"

"Nina gave it to me a while ago. Sometimes I'll have clients who request grooming services, and I arrange to pick up or drop off. If it's after hours, I need the code so I can bring them into the kennels in the back."

"I see," Owen said encouragingly.

Marla lifted a shoulder and sighed. "I knew Beau was there, and I just had this idea to take him—just temporarily—to teach Camille a lesson."

"And what was the plan once you had him?" Owen asked.

She frowned. "Well, I'm not proud of this, but I thought Camille owed me and I wanted to collect."

"Owed you what?" I asked, unable to hold my tongue.

"An apology, really. But I knew I'd never get that from her."

When she said nothing else, Owen prodded her. "An apology for what?"

"Camille and I had a fight several years back. I told you

this already. She cancelled last minute, and I kept her deposit."

Owen shook his head. "That seems understandable."

"It's standard procedure. But I guess since she thought she was special, she didn't believe my policies applied to her and her precious dog."

"So she was angry," Owen said.

"And then some," Marla confirmed. "As I already told you, she began telling anyone who would listen that my kennels were unsanitary and that dogs would get sick there. I lost half my business overnight. She was very influential in the dog world."

"But she never apologized?" I guessed.

"She did not. And she cost me my reputation. Not to mention a great deal of money."

"Is that why you decided to ransom Beau? For money?" Owen asked.

Marla bit her lip. "Er..."

"We saw the text on her phone," he said.

"Yes. That's why." Marla didn't say anything else for a moment, and Owen and I exchanged a look.

"Marla, when you entered the Paw Spa that night, was anyone else inside?"

"Just Beaumont Royale," she said.

"And no one else had entered when you left?" I asked.

She shook her head. "If you're suggesting I might have hurt Camille... I would never do anything like that. Forcing her to repay a moral debt is one thing... but I'd never kill anyone!" These last words were hissed as if the idea was too horrific to give voice to.

"Thank you, Marla. That's what we needed to know." Owen stood, and I followed his lead.

In the corridor, he paused. "Anything I missed in there?"

I shook my head. "I don't think so. She confessed to the dognapping, explained her motive for the ransom, and since Victoria didn't mention Marla being in the spa when she arrived, I believe her when she says she left before they arrived."

"Me too."

"Let's have a talk with Nina," he said. "Just give me one second to chat with John about finalizing the charges against Marla."

I waited in the hallway, my mind spinning at Marla's decision to take out her anger at Camille by stealing her dog. If anyone took Taco from me, I didn't know what I'd do. I felt a bit naked being without him as it was, but he'd been spending so much time with Diantha, it was hard to resent her for it.

"You'll never guess who's here," Owen said as he stepped back through the steel door separating the hallway from the front of the station.

I was likely never going to guess, so I waited for him to tell me.

"Elliott Nazar," he said.

I thought about the notes in Camille's book under Elliott's name. They'd shed very little light on their relationship. More code, I guessed. Maybe Elliott could explain.

The thought of wrapping up every loose end all at once pleased me. "Should we chat with Nina first?"

Owen tilted his head and then gave it a little shake. "I'd actually like to chat with Mr. Nazar first." As he said this, John stepped down the hallway with Mr. Nazar in tow.

"Hello," Owen said.

Elliott looked between Owen and me as John disappeared into the interrogation room to get Marla. "Wait, you're the lady from the inn, aren't you?"

"I am," I agreed.

"Dahlia assists the Saltcliff police from time to time," Owen said, waving an arm toward his office door. "Why don't we chat in here?"

I led the way and Elliott followed, and he and I sat across from Owen at his desk.

"Thank you for coming in. You're a difficult man to track down," Owen said.

Elliott did not answer immediately, but after a moment of silence he said, "yes, I'm very busy. Well, I'm here now. What can I do for you?"

"Can you please tell us why you left town so suddenly earlier this week?" Owen asked.

Elliott's eyes swung to me. "You already have my deposit, which I knew you'd keep if I left. I'm not contesting it. You're hauling me into the police station—with a warrant—because I had to cut my hotel stay short?"

"What?" I was surprised by his question. "No, of course not."

"This is actually an inquiry more to determine if you might have had anything to do with an investigation we're pursuing at the moment," Owen informed him. "A murder."

"Camille Hawthorne," Elliott almost whispered.

"Right," I said.

Elliott sighed. "I was heartbroken about my friend Camille. I just couldn't judge the show after her death. It would have been too hard." Mr. Nazar delivered this little speech in a near-falsetto, and there was no question in my mind it was an act.

"What was your relationship with Camille Hawthorne?" Owen asked, ignoring the man's theatrics.

"We were very old friends. She helped me get my start in judging."

I nodded. That was what we'd already learned. "And you helped her in return?" I asked.

Elliott's eyes slid to mine, then he turned back to Owen. "We were friends. We helped each other. That is what friends do."

"How did you help Camille?" Owen asked.

"You know, this and that." Elliott crossed his arms and sat back, looking between us.

"Can I show you something?" Owen asked Elliott, sounding like a friend sitting across a table at a bar more than an investigator talking with a potential murder suspect.

"I don't guess I have much choice," Elliott said.

Owen produced Camille's book, opening it to the page flagged with Elliott's name. He read, "'Fake ID. False experience. History.' Does this make any sense to you?"

Elliott's eyes lingered on Camille's flowery handwriting, moving across the words over and over. His face colored slightly, but his eyebrows went up as he gave a dismissive shrug. "Who knows. The woman was eccentric."

"So you have no idea what this means? Fake ID? Why would Camille write that under your name?" Owen pressed.

Elliott remained silent.

Owen also remained silent.

I grew exceedingly uncomfortable.

Suddenly, Owen stood. He picked up the receiver on the phone on his desk, punched a button, and said, "John. Can you come do an ID verification for Mr. Nazar? My office." He hung up and turned to Nazar. "I'm just going to have John get your prints and copy your ID. We've got someone else we need to chat with, but we'll be back once he's finished with that."

John rapped at the door, and Owen nodded at me to follow him out.

Elliott Nazar said nothing.

"Let's chat with Nina," Owen said in the hallway. "You ready?"

"I guess so," I said, feeling like my day was suddenly on fast forward. Owen squeezed my hand gently, then released me and pulled open the door for me.

Inside, Nina Reyes waited at the table. She was drawn and pale and visibly shaking. I couldn't help feeling a little bit sorry for her.

She looked up at us, and then back down at the table.

"What happens now?" she asked quietly.

Owen and I sat. "What do you mean, Nina?" Owen asked her.

"You think I did it. You're sure I killed Camille. So what happens now? Prison?" Nina stared at the tabletop as she spoke.

Owen glanced at me his eyes wide with surprise. Had

she confessed? It had been rather anticlimactic, but I was relieved.

"Nina, are you admitting to the murder of Camille Hawthorne?" Owen asked, turning on the recording device and setting it on the table.

Nina looked between us and then dropped her eyes, sobbing silently. It wasn't really an answer.

"Let's take a few steps back," Owen said gently. "Before we talk about what happens next, let's talk about what happened the night Camille came into the Paw Spa after hours."

Nina sniffed and looked back up. "Okay," she said in a wobbly voice.

"We know that Marla Carver used a code to enter and take Beaumont Royale out the back door. That would have left the back door unlocked."

Nina nodded.

"Then, Camille and Victoria arrived and had an altercation."

Nina looked between us, a furrow between her brows. I didn't think she'd known this before.

"When Victoria left, Camille was unconscious. The next point in time we're sure about is when Derek arrived to find Camille in the tub, dead. I'm sure you can see that there are some questions between Camille being unconscious on the floor and Camille turning up dead in the tub."

And the back door had been unlocked the whole night if that's how Marla had left, I realized. Why hadn't I thought about that before? Clearly, Owen had.

Nina's eyes were wide as she stared at Owen.

"I'm asking you, Nina, if you have any knowledge of how Camille might have gotten from the floor to the tub."

Nina pulled her bottom lip between her teeth, and her eyes fluttered. "Can I ask you something?"

"Sure," Owen said, friendly as ever.

"The person who did this... will they... will they get locked up? Right away?"

Owen tilted his head to one side. "I can't say for sure. There could be bail, but... yes, they'd be held at least for a little while. But everyone has the right to bail."

Nina sniffled and swallowed. Then she gave a little nod, as if deciding to speak. "I did it. I killed her. I went in that morning and found her and carried her to the tub and drowned her. I was so mad at her and so tired of her holding things over my head. I just... I just held her down until she... you know."

Owen said nothing for a moment, and I assumed he was processing this information. But then something occurred to me.

"Nina," I said. "How did you lift her into the tub?" Nina was a small woman, maybe a hundred and ten pounds total. Camille wasn't big, but she'd been tall, sturdy. I'd guess she probably weighed at least one hundred and forty pounds. The tub had sides that were at least three and a half feet high. It would be difficult to maneuver that weight up and over and into the tub without quite a lot of effort, and I'd imagine Camille's body would have been pretty banged up as a result. But it was not.

Owen shifted his gaze to meet mine, a little smile lifting his lips on each side.

"Oh, it was difficult," Nina said. "I had to drag her and then kind of..." her voice cracked. "Kind of just, like..." tears rolled down her cheeks now as her voice warbled. "Shoved her in..."

I didn't believe her, but I didn't understand why she'd lie. This was the second confession we'd gotten. And I still didn't think we'd found the murderer.

Just then, a knock came at the door to the interrogation room. Owen rose to answer it and then looked back at me. "Dahlia? Let's step out for a moment."

In the hallway, John showed Owen a laptop screen. "Elliott Nazar did not exist before about ten years ago," John said. "But his fingerprints match a record here." He pointed to the screen.

"Samuel Haggerty. Charged with breaking and entering, theft, vandalism... he's got quite a record."

John nodded. "But the crimes stopped when he became Elliott."

"Interesting," Owen said. "Good work, John."

"What does that mean?" I asked Owen.

"I think I know what happened," Owen said. "And I think we're talking to the right people. Come on." He headed back to his office to talk to Elliott.

"Mr. Nazar," Owen said, sitting again. "Or do you prefer Haggerty?"

Elliott let out a breath and sagged in his chair. "Look, I needed to turn over a new leaf. I'm sure you saw the rap sheet."

Owen nodded. "And did Camille Hawthorne help you with the new leaf?"

Elliott scrubbed a hand over his jaw and nodded. "She did."

"How?" I asked, surprised Camille would involve herself with a criminal.

"Caught me in her house one night—actually her dog caught me."

"Why didn't she call the police?" I asked.

"You know what? I never was sure about that. But she didn't. Instead, she seemed impressed that I knew about her dog—fancy breed, a Borzoi. Beau's father—her previous dog. She asked me if I wanted to strike a deal or if I'd prefer she call the police."

"You took the deal," Owen said. "What was it?"

Nazar smiled then and shook his head. "One thing I'll say about that lady. She knew how to play the long game."

"What do you mean?" I asked.

"Told me she wanted to show her dog, but she didn't have the documentation required. She asked if I knew anyone in that world since I was clearly a criminal."

"I take it you did?" Owen asked.

Elliott shrugged.

"So what did she ask you to do?"

"She asked me to get papers for her dog, but she also said she'd pay to get new documentation for me—to totally scrub my identity and forge my background so I could qualify to become a judge at these fancy dog shows."

Owen let out a low whistle. "Sounds like kind of a long shot."

"You'd think, right?" Elliott sounded like he was settling into his tale. I wondered if he'd ever gotten to tell it before. "But this lady had money like you wouldn't believe, and she was determined. She got me all set up, gave me a stipend and an apartment, and got her dog his papers.

"She kept getting me gigs judging little shows, regional stuff, and she paid for me to fly and stay in hotels. Soon, I kind of forgot I wasn't actually Elliott Nazar, fancy dog show guy. I just became him. And in the meantime, she studded her dog and produced her first championship litter. That's where Beau came from."

I was beginning to understand that Camille Hawthorne was a far more patient woman than I'd guessed previously.

"By the time she was ready to show Beau, I'd had ten years of experience."

"And so you could judge his shows," Owen guessed.

"Correct."

"And you made sure Beau won?" I asked.

Elliott shrugged. "For a fee."

Owen and I exchanged a look. "You were blackmailing Camille?" he asked.

"Not exactly. I was just making sure if I was going to risk everything that it was worth it."

"And was it?" I asked. I couldn't imagine living with so many secrets.

Elliott stared at the desktop for a moment. "Not really. After a while I just wanted to be legit. I loved the dog show world—always have. I was the only kid growing up in south Chicago breaking into houses to watch cable broadcasts of dog shows I couldn't get at home."

It was an interesting story, that was for sure.

"Camille wouldn't let you go?" Owen guessed.

"She needed me, she said. And she threatened to expose me if I ever turned her down or told anyone."

"And did you? Ever tell anyone?" I asked.

He glanced up at me. "Only one person. My best friend. A woman I met on the circuit years ago."

"Why did you confide in her? Weren't you worried she'd tell someone?" Owen asked.

Nazar shrugged. "If you're gonna tell someone a secret, make sure they have secrets of their own."

Owen nodded then, and I suspected we were both thinking the same thing.

"Elliott, can you account for your whereabouts the night Camille was killed at the Paw Spa?" Owen asked.

He frowned. "I was staying at her inn," he said, pointing at me. "So I guess she's my alibi."

I shook my head. "We don't ask guests to check in and out, or have electronic keys. And we don't have cameras on the doors. I can't verify anyone's whereabouts." Though, now that I thought about it, I should look into a security system with cameras. And maybe it was time to switch to electronic keys.

Elliott shrugged. "Then I guess you'll have to take my word for it."

"Maybe," Owen said, rising. "Dahlia, will you join me?"

We stepped into the hallway after Owen called John to come move Mr. Nazar to the other interrogation room.

"Is Nina his best friend?" I asked as soon as we were alone.

Owen grinned. "I'd bet my left hand on it."

We went back in to speak with Nina.

"Nina," Owen said, sitting down again. "Do you know Mr. Elliott Nazar?"

A strange look flashed across Nina's face. Alarm?

Guilt? "Yes," she said slowly. "I've known Elliott a long time."

"Did you see him the night of Camille Hawthorne's death?"

She looked between us. "No."

"Are you sure?" Owen asked. "If I checked your phone records, would I find an early morning call to Mr. Nazar's phone?"

"Maybe, I mean... I spoke to Elliott often." Nina looked distinctly uncomfortable now.

"Did you call him that morning?" Owen pressed.

"I don't remember! Everything happened so fast! Camille was wandering around, and then Beau was missing..."

"Wait," I said. "Camille was wandering around?"

"Er. No." Nina pressed her lips shut. Then her face crumpled and she sobbed into her hands for a moment.

My heart twisted. I felt sorry for her. "Nina?" I said.

She shook her head. "I promised him I wouldn't say anything... I just... I'm no good at any of this."

"At what, Nina? Promised who?" Owen's voice was gentle.

Nina wiped furiously at her eyes. "Elliott." She took a deep breath. "You're right. You already know that. I called him. Camille was inside the spa when I came in that morning early. She was wandering around, incoherent. I thought she must've unlocked the back door because it was unlocked when I came in—I didn't know about Marla and Beau. I just figured Camille had sent Beau home with Marva."

"Go on," Owen prodded.

"Well, Camille could barely walk, and there was blood all down her suit. I didn't know what to do. She barely seemed to realize I was there. She was practically incoherent. For a minute, if it wasn't for the blood, I thought maybe she was drunk."

"So you called Elliott Nazar?"

Nina nodded. "Elliott was one of my oldest friends. He knew about... you know. The thing in Santa Fe. And he understood. I'm guessing you know about Santa Fe? The schnauzer?"

Owen and I both nodded, confirming that we did.

"I figured. But Elliott... He knew and he didn't hate me, and so we were friends. I trusted him. And he knew Camille. So I called him. He told me to sit tight, and he'd be right there."

"So Elliott showed up. Then what?"

"I let him in the back door, and he went to talk to Camille. She wasn't any better by then, though. She was confused and kept passing out. I told him we needed to get her some help, but he convinced me we'd only look guilty if we did that. He said it was obvious someone else had been here, had tried to kill her. He convinced me that we should just finish what they started, make it look like they succeeded."

I shook my head. "Why?"

Nina sobbed for a moment and then pulled herself upright again. "Because she wouldn't hear reason. She had dirt on both of us, controlled us both with her information. And Elliott said this would put a stop to it for once and for all. That we'd finally be free."

"So you helped Elliott put her in the tub?"

Nina shook her head. "No. I told him I wouldn't do it. I tried to stop him, to make him think about it some more."

"So he did it himself?" I asked.

She shuddered. "And he told me if I ever told anyone, he'd kill me." She looked up at us with terrified, wild eyes.

"You're safe here, Nina," Owen said.

"Am I going to be in trouble?" she asked.

He frowned and thought quietly. "Might be," he answered. "But telling us the truth counts for something." Owen swung his blue-eyed gaze to me. "Let's step outside for a moment. Nina," he said to the woman crying miserably on her arms, "we'll be right back."

I rose to follow Owen, wishing Taco were with me so I could let him stay with Nina and calm her down a bit. I wasn't great at comforting people, but Taco was an expert.

We left Nina there at the table and went to confront Elliott.

Chapter Sixteen

Elliott sat stiffly at the table opposite Owen and me in interrogation room two. I was exhausted from the conversations we'd already had this morning, which were just as emotionally taxing as they were intellectually complex. Elliott did not look particularly well-rested, either. Dark circles ringed his eyes, and the green scarf wrapped around his long neck was wrinkled and stained, as if he'd been tugging at it.

"What would you prefer we call you at this point?" Owen asked him.

The man frowned and gazed at the worn linoleum tabletop for a moment before answering in a quieter voice than I'd heard from him. "Elliott, please. I've been him a long time now, and I don't think I want to go back to Sam's life."

"I understand," Owen said. "Change can be pretty

hard, and I imagine you've gotten used to being Elliott, and to life that's come with being an esteemed judge."

Elliott's eyes danced from my face to Owen's, and then back to the table. Was he checking to see if Owen was making fun of him? "I have."

"I guess having Camille hold all the keys to your past felt a bit like a threat to Elliott's identity, right?"

Elliott said nothing.

"What do you think, Dahlia? If I had information that could take away everything you'd worked hard for over the last ten years, would you want to keep me from sharing it?"

I knew Owen was using the question to try to get Elliott to talk, but I still thought for a moment before answering. "It would feel like a threat," I said. "And I'd be afraid all the time, I think. Constantly worrying that maybe whatever effort I made now, whatever success I had wouldn't matter because you could take it all away if you decided to."

Elliott looked up at me, his eyes wide with sympathy. "It's awful, I assure you," he said. "Especially if the person who holds all the cards constantly reminds you that she can expose you on a whim any time she feels like it."

"That would be very stressful," I said, happy I didn't really find myself in that situation.

"Always watching your back, always waiting for the axe to fall," Elliott went on.

"Of course," Owen agreed. "And I couldn't blame you

for wanting to find a way to make the threats stop, to put an end to the stress for once and for all."

Elliott gazed at him, but didn't deny that he felt this way.

"You must realize we've spoken to Nina," Owen went on. "The murder happened at her business, and she's very concerned about what that means for her future."

For a moment, no one spoke and the air in the room began to feel thicker and thicker as the tension—my tension, at least—grew.

"What did Nina say?" Elliott finally asked, his voice low.

"She told us what happened when she arrived at the Paw Spa the morning of Camille's death," Owen said.

Elliott waited, as if hoping Owen might share Nina's version of events with him so he could agree with or contradict them.

"I was hoping you'd tell us your version," Owen said.

"What makes you think I have a version?" Elliott asked. "I left town, remember?"

Owen nodded, but then he pulled something from his pocket and set it on the table. It was the single gold link Taco had discovered at the Paw Spa. "I think this is yours?"

Elliott frowned at the little piece of metal but said nothing.

"Your bracelet," I reminded him. "I saw it when you

checked in. I noticed it because it was so different from the rest of your aesthetic. Big, flashy."

Elliott appeared to be trying to will the link off the table, to make it vanish with his eyes. He was having no luck.

"We found it at the Paw Spa," I went on. "So we know you were there sometime between checking into the Inn and departing."

"This proves nothing," Elliott said.

"Do you have the bracelet Dahlia saw when you checked in at the inn?" Owen asked.

Elliott made a dismissive sound. "I'm not wearing it right now," he said.

"If I sent a few officers to your home to search, would they find it there? We can do that," Owen said. "It will delay things a bit. We'll need to get a warrant, and that takes a few days. We can give you a nice bed in the holding cell, though, if you'd like to wait."

Elliott's face turned darker, his cheeks flushing with color. "That isn't necessary," he said. After a long moment, he added, "it's mine."

"Wonderful," Owen said. "So now you can tell us how it got to the Paw Spa."

Elliott looked between us, anger flaring in his dark eyes, but after a moment, he blew out a breath and seemed to deflate. "Fine. I was there. Nina called me because she didn't know what to do when she found Camille wandering around and bleeding."

"Nina called you for help?" I asked.

Elliott's lips pressed into a line before he answered. "Yes. Or advice. She was upset, obviously. She asked me to come. We were friends. Had been for a while."

Owen nodded, encouraging Elliott to go on.

"I went in the back door, like she asked, and she was there with Camille, trying to get her to sit down. Camille was pretty out of her mind, though. She was half-hysterical, crying about Beau, though I'm not sure what she was saying. Her words were slurry, and she actually passed out a couple times. That's how I broke my bracelet."

"I don't understand," I said. "How did Camille passing out break your bracelet?"

Elliott sighed. "I caught her as she fell, and my arm caught on the door handle to the tub area. The bracelet caught and got pulled so hard all the links came apart." He looked sad as he said this, and scrubbed his gray goatee with one hand before leaning back in the chair.

"Go on," Owen suggested.

There was another long pause as Elliott thought about what he wanted to say next. Or maybe what he didn't want to say. He glanced between us, then his eyes rose to the ceiling. "I'd had enough, okay?"

"Enough?" I asked.

"Of being harassed and controlled. I'm a grown man.

And Nina! She made a mistake years ago, and she didn't deserve to have that woman constantly holding it over her head. It was too much. It needed to stop."

"So you..." Owen prodded.

"I finished what someone else clearly started. You need to understand, Camille was in a bad way to start with. She was bleeding from her head, she could barely stay conscious. She probably would have fallen in the tub herself."

"But she didn't, did she?" Owen asked.

Elliott blinked once, slowly. Then he looked at Owen and said, "No. She did not. I put her in the tub, and she drowned. Nina tried to convince me not to do it. This is not her fault."

"Did Nina physically try to stop you?" I asked. I wasn't sure why it seemed important.

Elliott glanced at me. "No, but she didn't exactly cheer me on, either."

"So you picked Camille up and put her in the tub?" Owen asked. "Did she struggle or ask you not to?"

"She was whacked out," Elliott said. "When I picked her up, she kind of just melted into my arms. She didn't fight me at all. I put her in the tub like a puppy, and then all I had to do was push her down a bit. It was almost like she wanted me to do it."

I doubted very much that Camille had been hoping Elliott would drown her, but I didn't argue.

"And then you left town? Weren't you worried Nina would take the blame?" Owen asked.

Elliott shrugged. "No. Someone else had already tried, from what we could see. The woman was a bloody mess. We figured you guys would track down whoever did that, and it would be over."

"We did," Owen said.

"Who was it?" Elliott asked, but Owen didn't answer. He thanked Elliott for his time, and shut off his recorder, tucking it back into his pocket.

"I imagine we will have some more questions, but John will be in soon to process you," Owen said.

"Process me? What does that mean?" Elliott sounded worried.

"Elliott Nazar, you are under arrest for the murder of Camille Hawthorne." After reading Elliott his Miranda rights, we left the room.

Out in the hallway, Owen and I each took a deep breath as we looked at one another.

"That was exciting," I said. "It was just like on television."

Owen grinned. "We make a pretty good team," he said.

"We do."

"I'll take it from here. Why don't you go home and get some rest? Or at least get back to running the inn, which is probably busy enough without the addition of police work! Remember, the Policeman's Ball is Friday."

"I haven't forgotten," I promised.

Owen smiled and one of his big, warm hands cupped my cheek for a second as his eyes met mine. A buzz of awareness jolted through me and nerves erupted in my stomach. Without thinking about it, I reached for him, and he stepped in close and kissed me gently before letting me go.

My head was still spinning as he said, "I'll call you later."

I walked back to the inn through the Saltcliff spring sunshine, feeling like everything in my life was just about perfect.

Chapter Seventeen

The week following the Saltcliff Annual Dog Show passed at a pace that felt like a welcome return to normal. Taco and I took morning walks, Diantha went back to school, and the inn was not stuffed to the gills with dogs and owners. Instead, we had four rooms filled with families and couples, who ate breakfast with us and then went off to explore the beautiful central coast.

If there were any murders, or any police activity, I wasn't made aware of it, and for that I was thankful.

On Wednesday, Diantha had given me an assignment to go to a formal shop in nearby Monterey, where she'd called ahead and told the store's manager what I might be looking for. Perhaps it wasn't the usual thing to have one's not-quite-teenaged niece making these kinds of arrangements, but I was thankful all the same.

"You'll be fine, Dahlia. It's a dress shop. What could go wrong?" Amal was trying to reassure me but asking me what could go wrong was only inviting me to become even more concerned that my efforts to find appropriate attire for the ball would somehow end disastrously.

"I'm sure you're right. I wish I could take Taco." I clutched the keys to the Fiat tightly in my hand before realizing they were beginning to dig uncomfortably into my flesh.

"I don't think he'd be very welcome in a high-end boutique," Amal said with a kind smile.

"Probably not." In general, I didn't like to go to places where Taco wouldn't be allowed. If it was the kind of place that couldn't see the merits of my very sweet, loyal friend, then I wasn't sure it was my kind of place anyway. But I did need a dress.

"Taco and I will wait here for you to come back. I am sure it will be fun."

I doubted very much that it would be fun. Shopping was one of those things I'd had a few negative experiences with, mostly because I just didn't really know how to interact with the salespeople at fancy shops. They often seemed overly interested in my efforts to find nicely fitting garments, when I really thought I'd do better if they just left me alone. But Diantha had made it clear that at a high-end dress boutique, I'd have some help, and that I should try to accept it graciously.

It was time to focus on the end goal. I wanted to look nice for Owen. In reality, I wanted to look much better than nice, but I was going to start with realistic expectations. So off to Formalwear on Figaro I went.

I parked in the little parking lot to one side of the shop and steeled myself. I was a grown woman. I could shop for a dress. This was not going to be a problem. With that internal reassurance, I locked the car and went in.

The shop was small, with racks hanging around the floor displaying a wide range of beautiful dresses. The colors were impressive and a bit overwhelming, and for a moment, I just stood, gaping and trying to get my bearings.

"Hello there. Are you Dahlia Vale?" A cheerful older woman with long, abundant gray wavy hair greeted me with a smile.

"I am," I told her.

"Wonderful," she said. "Right on time, too. Thanks for being so punctual."

I nodded at her. "Punctuality is important."

"It is," she agreed.

Well, so far so good.

I stood awkwardly, my bag over my shoulder, gazing around at the wild celebration of color in every direction. How did one start? Where should I look first? I took a tentative step forward, but the woman who'd greeted me stepped into my path.

"I'm Anne."

"Very nice to meet you," I said.

"I want to make your shopping experience perfect," she said.

I was not sure how to respond to such an extreme desire.

"If you'd like to browse and be left alone, that is perfectly fine. If you'd like me to show a few things in your size, that works too. I know you'll be attending the Policeman's Ball in San Francisco, is that right?"

"That is correct," I confirmed.

"Well, I've taken the liberty of putting a few things into a room for you to examine and perhaps try on. Your niece sent me your photo, told me your size, and suggested that you were somewhat conservative in dress. Of course, you are welcome to try anything in the store you like."

"Oh!" I looked around. I was overwhelmed, and when another woman came through the door and the bell sounded loudly, I made a decision. "I think I'll start with the dresses you've selected," I said.

"Perfect. Right this way." Anne led me to a dressing room in the corner with a locking door and walls that went all the way up to the ceiling and down to the floor. For some reason, once I was inside, looking at my reflection in the floor-length mirror, I felt better. I could hear Anne helping the other customer as I gazed at the selection of dresses she had pulled for me. There were several black gowns, a red one, two in shades of blue, and an emerald green dress that drew my eye.

This was perfect. I could try each in solitude, and the removal of sales pressure allowed me time to think and really consider each one. Anne had even put a pair of high heels in the dressing room in my size, so I could see the dresses with heels, which I would undoubtedly be wearing at the ball.

In the end, I selected the green dress that had caught my attention right off the bat. It had short, capped sleeves and a fitted bodice with a plunging V neckline. It was a bit deep, but I found that I could make it a little less revealing with a strategically placed safety pin. The entire dress was covered in sequins, but not the flashy dance recital kind. These were demure, sophisticated. The skirt fell to my ankles, swishing delightfully around the heels. It was perfect.

"You found one!" Anne sounded pleased when I emerged from my room with the gown in one hand.

"I did. This one is perfect."

"I'm so glad you love it."

Amal and Diantha gushed over me as I dressed for the Ball in my bedroom at the inn that Friday afternoon. Owen was picking me up at four to drive up to the city. We had two hotel rooms secured, and while Owen had suggested we could dress there, I felt more comfortable with Diantha and my best friend to help me.

"You look incredible, Aunt Dolly!" Diantha stood behind me, looking into the mirror into which I gazed.

"Fabulous," Amal agreed. "Your hair is perfect this way."

Amal had helped weave my shoulder-length hair into an elaborate updo and pushed more pins into it than I would likely ever be able to locate when it was time to take them out.

Diantha had finished my look with a necklace she pulled from her mother's jewelry box. I didn't often wear jewelry, but I had to admit, the dazzling choker was perfect.

"Keep the lipstick in your bag," my niece reminded me. "And touch it up now and then." Makeup had been a whole other thing—I rarely wore much at all, but Diantha had insisted on helping me "go big" for the evening. Amal kept her in line, ensuring that the finished look was more "date night" than "late night."

"Owen should be here any minute," Amal said, looking at her watch. "I'll go out front in case he's early."

I thanked her and then looked around my bedroom,

nerves jigging in my stomach and making me a bit woozy. I'd packed my overnight bag, and Amal had volunteered to stay over with Diantha. There was nothing left for me to do.

"You'll feed Taco?" I asked Diantha.

Taco, who'd been laying on his bed near the window, lifted his head, ever interested in conversations about food.

"Of course," she said. "We'll handle everything. You just have fun."

"I will try. It feels odd to go without him."

"You already talked to the catering manager. No legumes at all," Diantha reminded me.

I looked at my loyal dog. It would be easier not to have him with me tonight, but it still felt like a risk. I had packed my EpiPen in my purse, and Owen knew exactly what to look for... Plus, the catering manager had assured me that the chicken dish I'd ordered didn't have legumes in it. "Okay."

I pulled the black shawl I'd found in Daisy's closet around my shoulders and picked up the bag, then went over to say goodbye to my dog.

"Be good, buddy," I told him, rubbing his velvet ears and kissing his nose. "Take care of Danny and Amal."

Taco grinned at me.

"Let's go," Diantha said, handing me the tiny, bejeweled purse she'd extracted from the depths of one of the dresser drawers.

In the lobby, Owen stood with his back to the apartment door, speaking with Amal. When I stepped out, he turned, and I felt my nerves jump into double-time. He looked incredible in his dress uniform. The dark color highlighted the incredible blue of his eyes and made his golden skin glow. But I didn't get a chance to tell him because he spoke first.

"Dahlia, you look amazing. So beautiful." Owen smiled broadly and stepped close, taking my bag from my hand and kissing my cheek. "This dress sets off your eyes perfectly," he said. "It's just... wow." A flush crept into Owen's cheeks, and I realized he might be nervous too.

"You look very handsome," I told him.

Diantha and Amal were looking on as if they'd bought tickets to this show, and I was eager to be on the way and out from under scrutiny. "Should we go?"

Owen nodded. "We probably should. It's a bit of a drive and we don't want to miss cocktail hour."

"Go, go," Amal said, herding us out the door. "Everything will be fine here. Have fun."

I gave Diantha a hug and a kiss on the forehead, and then headed out to Owen's car.

As soon as we were driving, just the two of us, all the awkwardness and nervousness fell away. It was always like that with us—we just fit. He didn't make me worry that I might say or do the wrong thing, and I never felt uncomfortable around him.

We dropped our bags into our respective rooms, and met again in the lobby where Owen escorted me to the ballroom where the ball was being held. We sipped cocktails and mingled, Owen's hand always on my low back or holding my own. He introduced me to his friends and colleagues, and I felt a rush of pride for him and the life he'd made for himself, the cause he served. Dinner was formal, and we sat with other couples and drank wine, and then, as the evening wore on, the music came up and the lights dimmed.

"Dahlia, will you dance with me?" Owen stood and held out a hand as a slow song played and the lights sparkled all around the ballroom.

I nodded, taking his hand and following him to the dance floor. Dancing was not my strong suit, but this ended up being much more like an extended hug, and I enjoyed every second of feeling Owen's warm arms around me, his reassuring presence surrounding me.

It was quite late when we finally gathered our things and headed out to the elevators.

"I had a wonderful time tonight," I told him. "I had no idea what to expect, but everything was perfect."

"I knew it would be when you agreed to come with me," he said. "Now I'll walk you to your room, if that's okay with you."

"It is." We rode in the elevator, hand in hand, and

walked slowly down the hallway to my door, which was a few down from Owen's room.

"Good night, Dahlia. Thank you for coming with me." Owen squeezed my hand, and I responded by giving his a tug.

He stepped closer, his eyes searching mine, and then leaned in and kissed me gently. I wrapped my arms around him, loving the way it felt to be held by him, to be kissed by him.

It felt like hours that we stood there like that, kissing and holding each other under the dim hallway lights. Finally, Owen pressed his forehead to mine. "I'm going to say goodnight now. But I hope you'll be up for a big breakfast and a little time wandering around the city tomorrow."

Warmth and happiness filled every part of me. "I will be." I lifted my head and looked into the blue eyes I knew I loved. "Goodnight, Owen. Thank you for everything."

He kissed my cheek and then turned away, and I slid the key card into my door and disappeared inside, my whole body tingling with warmth and contentment.

Chapter Eighteen

Coming back to Saltcliff felt like coming home in a way I'd never really experienced before. As I sat beside Owen, pleasantly full after a morning of tea and pancakes, salt air and city sights, I watched the deep blue Pacific roll by out the window. The sun flashed on the surface like a lamp, and the air glimmered with spring diamonds. California, and the Central Coast especially, were like no place I'd ever been before, and as we crested the little hill that took us inland and then down into Saltcliff's winding streets, I thought about how exceptionally lucky I was to call this place my home now.

I missed my sister, but Daisy had given me so much, and feeling grateful for friends, family, and a sense of purpose I'd never had before made me feel close to her too.

Owen pulled up in front of the inn and parked, grinning at me as he helped me out the passenger side. "Thanks for coming," he said. "I had a great time."

I took my bag after he lifted it out of the trunk, the green dress carefully hung in a garment bag, which he draped over one arm. "I'm sure the ball is always fun," I said.

"To be honest, I often skip it," he told me as he shut the trunk of the car. "I've never had anyone I wanted to take, and it seems like such a couples thing."

It had been. There were very few single people at the party. "Well, I'm flattered."

"But hopefully not surprised," he said. "You must feel it too, don't you? How easy things are when we're together? How well we just... fit?"

I did, but it made me happy to hear Owen say it. "I do," I told him.

"Good," he said.

We walked up the front walk and Owen gave me a kiss at the door, as if he was just delivering me home at the end of a date, which in a way he was. "I'll call you later," he said.

"Okay. Bye, Owen. I..." words nearly tumbled out of my mouth that I'd never said before. To anyone. But I caught them. I wasn't sure it was time. "I had a great time," I said instead.

Inside the lobby, I found Amal dusting the shelves, but

as soon as she heard me come in, she abandoned the task. "Tell me everything!"

I did, as best I could, pouring myself a cup of tea and the two of us settling on the couch before the fireplace. Taco had rushed to my side the second I'd entered, and now sat with his head on my lap, making his deep happy rumble while I petted his head.

"It sounds magical," she said. "And there was no... pressure?"

I shook my head. "None at all." I was lucky in that way too, Owen respected my boundaries. Completely.

"He's so amazing. You're really lucky to have found him."

"I am," I said, thinking about the moment at the door. "I think I might be in love with him."

Amal clapped her hands in front of her happily. "That's wonderful!"

We had spent an awful lot of time talking about me over the past weeks, and I knew Amal was grappling with her decision over her cousin's wedding.

"Have you made any decisions about going home?" I asked her.

Amal's smile dropped and she sighed. "I think I have to go," she said.

"You don't look happy."

"I'm so torn. I was going to say no, but then my mother called. Her sister is quite sick, and she guilted me into promising to come home since it's probably the last time I'll see her."

"The aunt who isn't happy with you?" I asked.

Amal inclined her head. "That's the one. She disagreed with everything about who I am, how I live my life."

I understood. For a very traditional person, it was possible that a woman moving to another country, living independently, and loving another woman might be difficult to comprehend. "Maybe she will have had time to think about it?"

"Or to let her hatred fester and grow," Amal said darkly.

It was possible. But I knew people could change. I'd changed a lot myself. "I'm glad you're going to go."

"I hope I'll feel glad before I actually have to leave."

"When is it?" I asked.

"I've put it on the calendar at the desk. I leave in two weeks, and I'll be gone two weeks."

Two weeks without Amal. I would miss her, I realized. So would Diantha. "We will miss you," I said, voicing my thoughts. "But we will be living vicariously through your exciting travels."

"I'll do my best to make them exciting, then. I fear there will be a lot of sitting around with family. And a lot of food."

"We like food," I reminded her.

Amal laughed and we each sipped our tea. As with Owen, Amal was easy to be around. She accepted me just as I was, and made me feel at home. I was lucky.

When Diantha returned from school, she dropped her bag just inside the inn's door and flung herself at me, giving me the biggest hug I'd ever received.

"Aunt Dolly! I missed you!"

I hugged my niece, surprised at the tears that jumped into my eyes. No one had ever missed me like this, I didn't think. It was overwhelming.

Taco thought this was a great chance to do some jumps and spins, and he zoomed around the lobby before I managed to get his attention.

"Taco, calm down."

"Sorry," Diantha said with a sheepish smile. "I was so excited to see you, it must've been contagious." She dropped to Taco's side and petted his big head. "Sorry about that, boy. Didn't mean to get you in trouble."

I took a deep breath and blew it out, feeling satisfaction trickle through every cell inside me. I'd understood the concept of happiness before, but for the first time in my life, I was sure I felt it too.

Saltcliff B&B Vanilla Chai Scones

Saltcliff B&B Vanilla Chai Scones Recipe (Yields 10 scones)

Warm and cozy, these scones are a favorite of Dahlia's guests, and one of my favorite things to make on weekends!

Dry Ingredients:

- 2 ½ cups (312g) all-purpose flour
- ¼ cup (50g) granulated sugar
- 2 ½ tsp baking powder (*reduce to 2 tsp for high altitude*)
- ½ tsp baking soda
- ½ tsp salt
- 1 tsp ground cinnamon
- ¼ tsp ground cardamom
- ¼ tsp ground ginger
- ⅛ tsp ground cloves

- ⅛ tsp ground nutmeg
- *Optional:* zest of 1 orange for brightness

Cold Ingredients:

- ½ cup (113g) unsalted butter, cold and cubed
- ⅔ cup (160ml) heavy cream (*increase by 1 tbsp for high altitude*)
- 1 large egg
- 2 tsp vanilla bean paste (*or 1 tbsp pure vanilla extract*)
- 1 tbsp brewed strong chai tea (*or milk for richer flavor*)

Optional Glaze (for more vanilla flavor):

- ½ cup powdered sugar
- 1–2 tbsp milk or chai tea
- ½ tsp vanilla extract

Instructions:
1. Preheat Oven:

- **Sea level:** 400°F
- **High altitude:** 390°F
- Line a baking sheet with parchment paper.

2. Dry Mix:

Whisk together flour, sugar, baking powder, baking soda, salt, and all spices in a large bowl.

3. Cut in Butter:

Add cold butter and work into the flour with a pastry cutter or fingertips until pea-sized crumbs form.

4. Wet Mix:

In another bowl, whisk cream, egg, vanilla bean paste, and brewed chai (or milk).

5. Combine:

Pour wet mixture into dry ingredients and stir until a shaggy dough forms. Knead briefly on a floured surface until just combined.

6. Shape:

Form into a 1-inch thick round. Cut into 10 wedges or use a round cutter.

Tip: Chill shaped scones for 10 minutes before baking for crisp edges and taller rise.

7. Bake:

Place on baking sheet and optionally brush tops with cream and sprinkle sugar.

Bake **18–22 minutes** (check at 17 min for high altitude) until golden. Cool on wire rack.

8. Optional Glaze:

Whisk glaze ingredients and drizzle over cooled scones.

Zucchini Carrot Raisin Protein Quick Bread

Zucchini Carrot Raisin Protein Quick Bread

Dahlia and I share an interest in maintaining muscle mass as we age in order to remain strong and capable for as long as possible. To do this, we're starting to focus more on getting enough protein in our diets, something many people don't manage on a daily basis. Here's a sneaky way to add some protein (and vegetables!) to a tasty treat.

Ingredients:

Dry:

- 1 cup all-purpose flour (*increase by 2-3 tbsp for high altitude*)
- ½ cup whole wheat flour
- 1 scoop (about 30g) vanilla whey protein powder (*or plant-based vanilla protein*)
- 1 ½ tsp ground cinnamon

- ½ tsp ground ginger
- ¼ tsp nutmeg
- 1 tsp baking soda (*reduce to ¾ tsp for high altitude*)
- ½ tsp salt

Wet:

- 2 large eggs
- ⅓ cup melted coconut oil (or neutral oil)
- ¼ cup maple syrup or honey
- ¼ cup brown sugar
- ½ cup unsweetened applesauce (*add an extra tbsp for high altitude*)
- 1 tsp vanilla extract

Add-ins:

- 1 cup grated zucchini (squeeze moisture out slightly)
- ¾ cup grated carrot
- ½ cup raisins (or chopped dates)
- ¼ cup chopped walnuts or pecans (optional)

Instructions:

1. Preheat Oven to 350°F (177°C) (*Decrease to 340°F (171°C) for high altitude*)

Grease or line a **9x5 loaf pan** with parchment paper.

2. Mix Dry:

In a large bowl, whisk together flours, protein powder, baking soda, spices, and salt.

3. Mix Wet:

In another bowl, beat eggs with oil, maple syrup, sugar, applesauce, and vanilla until smooth.

4. Combine:

Add wet mixture to dry. Stir until just combined (don't overmix).

Fold in zucchini, carrot, raisins, and nuts.

5. Bake:

Pour into prepared loaf pan. Smooth the top.

Bake for **45–55 minutes** or until a toothpick comes out clean. (*High altitude tip: Check at 42 minutes. If top is browning too fast, loosely tent with foil.*)

Cool in pan 10 minutes, then transfer to wire rack.

Allergen Notes:

- Contains gluten, eggs, and dairy (from whey).
- Nut-free if you skip walnuts/pecans.
- For dairy-free: use plant protein instead of whey.

Lemon Poppyseed Muffins
(Makes 12)

**Lemon Poppyseed Muffins (Makes 12)
Ingredients:**

- 1 ¾ cups (220g) all-purpose flour (*Add 1 tbsp extra for high altitude*)
- ¾ cup (150g) granulated sugar
- 2 tbsp poppy seeds
- 2 tsp baking powder
- ¼ tsp baking soda (*reduce to ⅛ tsp at high altitude*)
- ¼ tsp salt
- Zest of 2 lemons
- ⅔ cup plain Greek yogurt (full-fat or 2%)
- ½ cup (120ml) neutral oil (like canola or vegetable)
- 2 large eggs

- ¼ cup fresh lemon juice (*Increase by 1 tbsp for high altitude*)
- 1 tsp vanilla extract
- 1–2 tbsp milk, as needed to loosen batter (optional)

Instructions:

1. Preheat oven to 400°F *(or 375°F high altitude)*.

Line a 12-cup muffin tin with paper liners or grease well.

2. Dry mix:

In a large bowl, whisk together flour, sugar, poppy seeds, baking powder, baking soda, salt, and lemon zest.

3. Wet mix:

In a separate bowl, whisk together yogurt, oil, eggs, lemon juice, and vanilla until smooth.

4. Combine:

Add wet ingredients to dry and stir just until combined. If batter is too thick, add 1 tbsp milk to loosen.

5. Scoop & Bake:

Fill muffin cups about ¾ full.

Bake for **16–18 minutes**, or until a toothpick comes out clean and tops are lightly golden. (*Check at 14 for high altitude*).

Cool in the pan 5 minutes, then transfer to a rack.

Allergen Notes:

- Contains gluten and eggs.
- Dairy from yogurt (can sub with coconut or almond yogurt).
- Nut-free unless using flavored yogurt with nut content.

More Nancy

Join my newsletter at nancystewartauthor.com

The Saltcliff Mystery Series:

Book 1: Keeled Over at the Cliffside

What happens when Gilmore Girls meets Murder, She Wrote? You get Dahlia Vale and snarky Diantha along with Taco Dog solving murders in the Saltcliff Mystery series! Follow along as Dahlia builds her community and family, and solves mysteries along the way. You'll love the small town vibe, B&B setting, and romantic sub-plot in this cozy culinary series!

Other Books - Steamy Small Town Romance written as Delancey Stewart

The Wilcox Wombats Series:

Book 1: The Wedding Winger

Ready for some ha ha with your hockey? The Wilcox Wombats bring the camaraderie and sense of found family you're looking for, along with snort-laughs and swoons. The first book features a star winger planning for his future, but caught up in the past. When his high school touch (the smart girl who always thought he was just a dumb jock) moves back next door, he knows he's in trouble. Grab it here!

The Kasper Ridge Series:

Free Prequel: Only a Summer

Book 1: Only a Fling

Read the Kasper Ridge Series to get your fill of small town steam with plenty of humor! Former fighter pilots share deep bonds and plenty of inside jokes. Step into their world as they join together to help renovate the Kasper Ridge Resort, a dilapidated mountain property in Colorado, left as an inheritance to Ghost, one of their own. But the inheritance also comes with a treasure hunt! Each book follows a different couple but each story builds another link in the hunt, so read them in order! Start with Only a Summer, which is free! Then pick up Only a Fling here.

The Singletree Series:

Book 1: Happily Ever His

What happens when the totally normal sister of a movie starlet meets her ultimate movie star crush, only to find out he is dating her famous sister? But it gets a bit more complicated than that.

Tess's sister has brought movie hottie Ryan home for her grandmother's 90th birthday to show the world how quickly she could move on after her very public divorce. The relationship is just for show... but Tess doesn't know that at first. And Gran? Is a video gaming, weed smoking, take-no-prisoners firecracker who tells it like it is. Toss in a lovesick chicken, and you're on your way to understanding what kind of series Singletree promises to be. Plan to laugh. Pick up book 1 here!

The MR. MATCH Series:

Free Prequel: Scoring a Soulmate

Book 1: Scoring the Keeper's Sister

If you enjoy a side of sports with your sexy men, and want both wrapped up in a hilarious package, then you're going to love Mr. Match. Soccer star and genius Max Winchell has discovered the formula for love and built a dating app around it. Though he keeps his identity secret, he convinces all his teammates to try it... and one after another, they fall in love. First up? Fernando "the fire" Fuerte, who shares an enemies-to-lovers romance with PR rep Erica, who happens to be his teammates twin sister. Taboo, forced proximity, and tons of witty banter up the steam in this one! Get it here!

The KINGS GROVE Series:

Book 1: When We Let Go

Coming right up, a bit of Sequoia mountain steam mixed with small town swoon! Head to Kings Grove for quirky side characters, emotional love stories, happy ever afters, and a cast you'll want to make your neighbors. Book 1 features Maddie returning to her childhood home, only to be swept off her feet by a handsome and potentially dangerous stranger. These books are steamy and engaging, with a touch of humor. Read book 1 here!

THE GIRLFRIENDS OF GOTHAM Series:

Book 1: Men and Martinis

Head to to the dot-com heyday of NYC - the late 1990s! Join Natalie Pepper as she makes her way in the big city in this Carrie

Bradshaw meets Bridesmaids coming of age story. Meet the girlfriends here!

The Digital Dating Series (with Marika Ray):

Book 1: Texting with the Enemy

Looking for sweet romance with a romcom kick? That's what you get when Delancey and Marika Ray team up! In this series starter, Elle is texting a guy she isn't sure she likes, but boy does he give good text. The only problem? She's actually texting her boss since "the guy" gave her his buddy's number instead of his own. Now she's falling slowly in love with the perfect guy and can't figure out why he doesn't seem perfect in person... Needless to say, hilarity ensues. Pick it up here!

www.ingramcontent.com/pod-product-compliance
Lightning Source LLC
Chambersburg PA
CBHW070454200726
48293CB00007B/2194